SNOBBERY
WITH
VIOLENCE

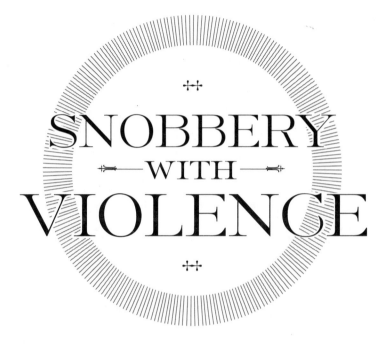

SNOBBERY
— WITH —
VIOLENCE

MARION CHESNEY

ST. MARTIN'S MINOTAUR 🦋 NEW YORK

SNOBBERY WITH VIOLENCE. Copyright © 2003 by Marion Chesney. All rights reserved. Printed in the United States of America. No part of this book may be used or reproduced in any manner whatsoever without written permission except in the case of brief quotations embodied in critical articles or reviews. For information, address St. Martin's Press, 175 Fifth Avenue, New York, N.Y. 10010.

www.minotaurbooks.com

Library of Congress Cataloging-in-Publication Data

Chesney, Marion.
    Snobbery with violence / Marion Chesney.—1st ed.
        p.   cm.
    ISBN 0-312-30451-X
    1. Private investigators—Great Britain—Fiction.   2. Aristocracy (Social class)—Fiction.   I. Title.

PR6053.H4535S66   2003
823'.914—dc21

                                                    2003041351

First Edition: July 2003

10 9 8 7 6 5 4 3 2 1

＋

For my husband, Harry, and my son, Charlie
With Love

＋

Sapper, Buchan, Donford Yates, practitioners in that school of Snobbery with Violence that runs like a thread of good-class tweed through twentieth-century literature.

—ALAN BENNET

SNOBBERY
WITH
VIOLENCE

ONE

All the world over, I will back the masses against the classes.

–WILLIAM EWART GLADSTONE

Unlike White's or Brooks's, it was simply known as The Club, lodged in a Georgian building at the bottom of St. James's Street, hard by St. James's Palace. Its membership was mostly comprised of the younger members of the aristocracy, who considered it a livelier place than the other stuffy gentlemen's clubs of London.

Some of them felt that the acceptance of Captain Harry Cathcart into The Club was a grave mistake. When he had left for the Boer War, he had been a handsome, easygoing man. But he had returned, invalided out of the army, bitter, brooding and taciturn, and he seemed unable to converse in anything other than clichés or grunts.

One warm spring day, when a mellow sun was gilding the sooty buildings and the first trembling green leaves were appearing on the plane trees down the Mall, Freddy Pomfret and Tristram Baker-Willis entered The Club and looked with deep disfavour on the long figure of the captain, who was slumped in an armchair.

"Look at that dismal face," said Freddy, not bothering to

lower his voice. "Enough to put a fellow off his dinner, what?"

"Needs the love of a bad woman," brayed Tristam. "Eh, Harry. What? Rather neat that, don't you think? Love of a bad woman, what?"

The captain, by way of reply, leaned forward, picked up the *Times* and barricaded himself behind it. He wanted peace and quiet to think what to do with his life. He lowered his paper once he was sure his tormentors had gone. A large mirror opposite showed him his reflection. He momentarily studied himself and then sighed. He was only twenty-eight and yet it was a face from which any sign of youth had fled. His thick black hair was showing a trace of grey at the temples. His hard and handsome face had black heavy-lidded eyes which gave nothing away. He moved his leg to ease it. His old wound still throbbed and hurt on the bad days, and this was one of them.

He was the youngest son of Baron Derrington, existing on his army pension and a small income from the family trust. His social life was severely curtailed. On his return from the war, he had been invited out to various dinner parties and dances, but the invitations faded away as he became damned as a bore who rarely opened his mouth and who did not know how to flirt with the ladies.

He put the *Times* back down on the table in front of him, and as he did so, he saw there was a copy of the *Daily Mail* lying there. Someone must have brought it in, for The Club would never supply a popular paper. There was a photograph on the front of a suffragette demonstration in Trafalgar Square and an oval insert of a pretty young girl with the caption, "Lady Rose, daughter of the Earl of Hadshire, joined the demonstrators."

Brave girl, thought the captain. That's her social life ruined. He put the paper down again and forgot about her.

But Lady Rose was possessed of exceptional beauty and a large dowry, so a month later her parents felt confident that her support for the suffragettes would not be much of a barrier to marriage. After all, the very idea of women getting the vote was a joke, and so they had told her, in no uncertain terms. They had moved to their town house in Eaton Square and lectured their daughter daily on where her duty lay. A season was a vast expense and England expected every girl to do her duty and capture a husband during it.

Normally, the independently-minded Lady Rose would have balked at this. She had been refusing a season, saying it was nothing more than a cattle market, when, to the delight of her parents, she suddenly caved in.

The reason for this was because Lady Rose had met Sir Geoffrey Blandon at a pre-season party and had fallen in love—first love, passionate all-consuming love.

He appeared to return her affections. He was rich and extremely handsome. Lady Rose was over-educated for her class, and her obvious contempt for her peers had given her the nickname The Ice Queen. But to her parents' relief, Sir Geoffrey appeared to be enchanted by their clever daughter. Certainly Rose, with her thick brown hair, perfect figure, delicate complexion and large blue eyes, had enough attributes to make anyone fall for her.

But the fact was that her support for the suffragettes had indeed damaged her socially, and it seemed as if Sir Geoffrey had the field to himself. Resentment against Rose was growing in the gentlemen's clubs and over the port at dinner parties after the ladies had retired. Suffragettes were simply men-haters. They needed to be taught a lesson. "What that gal needs," Freddy Pomfret was heard to remark, "is some rumpy-pumpy."

As the season got underway and social event followed social event, the earl began to become extremely anxious. He felt that by now Sir Geoffrey should have declared his intentions.

One day at his club, he met an old friend, Brigadier Bill Handy, and over a decanter of port after a satisfying lunch, the earl said, "I'd give anything to know if Geoffrey means to pop the question."

The brigadier studied him for a long moment and then said, "I think you should be careful there. Blandon's always been a bit of a rake and a gambler. Tell you what. Do you know Captain Cathcart?"

"Vaguely. Only heard of him. Sinister sort of chap who never opens his mouth?"

"That's the one. Now he did some undercover work behind the lines in the war. You mustn't mention this."

"I'm a clam."

"All right. Here's what I'll do. I'll give you my card and scribble something on the back of it. I'll give you his address. Pop round there and ask him to check up on Blandon. It's worth it. Rose is your only daughter. They say she talks like an encyclopaedia. Wouldn't have thought that would fascinate Blandon. How did you come to make such a mistake?"

"Not my fault," said the earl huffily. "My wife got her this governess and left the instruction to her."

"I hear that Lady Rose is a member of the Shrieking Sisterhood," remarked the brigadier, using the nickname for the suffragettes.

"Not any more, she ain't," said the earl. "Mind you, I think the only reason she lost interest was because of Blandon."

"Well, maybe there is something to be said for love, though I don't hold with it. A girl should marry background and money.

They last, love don't. Here's my card." He wrote an address down and handed it over.

The earl put his monocle in his eye and studied it. "I say, old man. Chelsea? No place for a gentleman."

"If Captain Cathcart were the complete gentleman he wouldn't dream of doing your snooping for you. But you'll be safe with him."

Lady Rose was at that moment fretting under the ministrations of her lady's maid. Having abandoned the Sisterhood—but only briefly, she told herself—Rose had once more subjected herself to the stultifying dress code of Edwardian society. While she had been supporting the suffragette movement, she had worn simple skirts and blouses and a straw hat. But now she was dressed in layers of silk underclothes, starched petticoats and elaborate gowns with waterfalls of lace. Her figure was too slim to suit the fashion of ripe and luscious beauty, and so art was brought to bear to create the small-waisted, S-shaped figure. A beauty had to have an outstanding bust and a noticeable posterior. Rose was lashed into a long corset and then put into a Dip Front Adjuster, a waist-cinch that stressed the fashionable about-to-topple-over appearance. Her bottom was padded, as was her bust. By the time the maid had slung a rope of pearls around Rose's neck and decorated the bosom of her gown with brooches, Rose felt she looked like a tray in a jeweller's window.

Geoffrey always praised her appearance but had implied that once she was married, she would be free to wear more comfortable clothes. Rose stared at the mirror as the maid put in pompadours, the pads over which her long hair would be drawn up and arranged. Sir Geoffrey had said nothing about when *we* are married. But he had stolen a kiss, just the other night, behind a pillar in the Jessingtons' ballroom, and stealing a kiss was tantamount to a proposal of marriage.

The captain lived in a thin white house in Water Street, off the King's Road. The earl fervently hoped that the man was a gentleman and not some sort of Neverwazzer who wore a bowler hat or carried a coloured handkerchief in his breast pocket or—horror upon horrors—brown boots with a dark suit. He had never met him but had heard about him in the clubs.

The earl climbed stiffly down from his carriage and waited while his footman rapped at the door. To his relief, the earl saw that the door was opened by a sober-looking gentleman's gentleman who took the earl's card, carefully turned down at one corner to show the earl was calling in person, put it on a silver tray, and retreated into the house.

The earl frowned. His title should have been enough to grant him instant admission.

The captain's servant returned after only a few moments and spoke to the footman, who sprinted down the stairs to tell the earl that the captain would be pleased to receive him.

The earl was ushered into a room on the ground floor. He was announced, and a tall saturnine man who had been sitting in a chair by the window rose to meet him.

"May we offer you something?" asked Captain Cathcart. "Sherry?"

"Fine, fine," mumbled the earl, taken aback by the amount of books in the shelves lining the room. His Majesty, King Edward, set such a good example by not opening a book from one year's end to another. Why couldn't everyone follow such a fine example?

"Sherry, Becket," said the captain to his manservant. And to the earl, "Do sit down, sir. I see the sun has come out at last."

"So it has," said the earl, who hadn't noticed. "I come on a delicate matter." He handed over the brigadier's card.

"What matter?"

"Well, y'see—" The earl broke off as the manservant re-entered the room with glasses and decanter on a tray. He poured two glasses and handed one to the captain and one to the earl.

"That will be all," said the captain and Becket noiselessly retreated.

The captain turned his fathomless black gaze on the earl, wondering why he had come. The earl was a small round man dressed in a frock-coat and grey trousers. He had a round, reddish face and blue eyes which had a childlike look about them.

"It's like this," said the earl, feeling awkward and embarrassed. "I have a daughter, Rose . . ."

"Ah, the suffragette."

"I thought people had forgotten about that," said the earl. "Anyway, Rose is being courted by Sir Geoffrey Blandon. He's not an adventurer. Good family. Nothing wrong there."

"And the problem?"

"He hasn't proposed. Rose is my only child. Would like some discreet chap to check up on Blandon. Find out if he's the thing. I mean, does he have a mistress who might turn awkward? That sort of business."

Having got it out, the little earl turned scarlet with embarrassment and took a gulp of sherry.

"I am not much out in the world these days," said the captain, "but knowing how gossip flies about, I would have thought if there was anything unsavoury about the man, you'd have heard it."

"Blandon's been in America for the past four years, came back in time for this season. Might be something nobody knows about. Handy says he's a gambler."

Captain Cathcart studied him for a long moment and then said, "A thousand pounds."

"What, what?" gabbled the earl.

"That is my fee for research and discretion."

The earl was shocked. This captain was a baron's son and yet here he was asking for money like a tradesman. And yet, why hadn't Blandon declared his intentions? He was spoiling Rose's chances of finding another suitor.

The captain let the silence last. A carriage rattled over the cobbles on the street outside and a small fire crackled on the hearth. A clock on the mantel ticked away the minutes.

"Very well," said the earl with a cold stare.

"In advance," said the captain mildly.

The earl goggled at him. "You have my word."

The captain smiled and said nothing.

The earl capitulated. "I'll give you a draft on my bank."

"You may use my desk."

The earl went over to a desk at the window and scribbled busily. He handed the draft to the captain and said angrily, "If there's nothing wrong, it'll be a waste of money."

"I should think to be reassured on the subject of your only daughter would be worth anything."

"Harrumph. I'm going. Report to me as soon as you can," snapped the earl.

The captain waited until Becket had ushered the earl out and then smiled at his manservant. "My coat and hat, Becket. I am going to the bank. I will have your overdue wages when I get back."

"That is most gratifying, sir."

At that moment, Rose was taking tea at the home of her mother's friend, Mrs. Cummings, in Belgrave Square. She looked dismally at the small butter stain on one of her kid gloves, and, for seemingly the hundredth time, damned the mad rules of society, one of which was that a lady should not remove her gloves when taking tea. Although the bread and butter had been carefully rolled, a spot had got onto one of her gloves. Most ladies avoided the problem by simply not eating. What insanity, thought Rose bitterly. She had a healthy appetite and the spread before her was of the usual staggering proportions. Apart from the bread-and-butter, there were ham, tongue, anchovy, egg-and-cress and foie gras sandwiches; chicken cutlets and oyster canapés. And then the cakes: Savoy, Madeira, Victoria and Genoa, along with French pastries, to be followed by petits fours, banana cream, chocolate cream and strawberry ice cream. And all of it sitting there mostly untouched so that the ladies would not soil their gloves.

Did no one but herself notice the poor on the streets of London? she wondered. And again she felt that uncomfortable feeling of isolation as she assumed she was probably the only person in society who did notice. Geoffrey, dear Geoffrey, did have some idea. He had told her that only the other day, the Duke of Devonshire had been visiting a bazaar with his agent and had stopped at a stall displaying wooden napkin rings and the duke had asked his agent what they were for.

"Napkin rings," said the agent. "Middle-class people keep them on the table to put their table napkins in between meals."

Said the astounded duke, "Do you mean that people actually wrap up their napkins and use them again for another meal?"

"Certainly," said the agent.

The duke gasped as he looked at the stall, "Good God!" he

exclaimed. "I never knew such poverty existed."

How Geoffrey had laughed at such idiocy. If only he would propose. She knew her parents were beginning to fret. She glanced at her mother, who was chatting amiably with her hostess. The countess had moaned before they had left for the tea party that she should never have allowed that "dreadful" governess to over-educate her child. What a world where intelligence was regarded with such deep suspicion. Poor Miss Tremp. Such a fine governess. She had moved on to another household. When I am married, I will take her out of servitude and make her my companion, thought Rose. And I will be married, she told herself firmly. The Duke of Freemount's ball was to take place the following week, the grandest affair of the season, and Geoffrey had whispered that he had something to ask her and he would put the question to her there. What else could he mean? But on the other hand, why had he not approached her father and asked permission to pay his addresses?

Harry Cathcart decided to start work right away. By dint of saying he had lost money to someone in a card game and he thought that someone might be Blandon, he managed to secure his address and a description of him. Blandon's apartment was in St. James's Square. Harry hired a closed carriage and sat a little way across the square to get a sight of his quarry. After a long wait, Blandon emerged. Although he was a fine figure of a man, Harry disliked him on sight. His stare was too arrogant, his eyes too knowing and his mouth too fleshy. There certainly was an air of the gambler about him.

First, Harry went to The Club and checked the betting book. There was nothing there. He frowned down at it. For the next few days, Harry tailed Sir Geoffrey. He found the man kept a mistress in Pimlico, but in these loose days would anyone consider the presence of a mistress a scandal? Perhaps Sir Geoffrey was not as rich as he was reported to be. Perhaps he was after Lady Rose for her money.

Harry could only just afford to keep up his membership of The Club. He could not afford to belong to any of the other London clubs.

He went back to his home and asked Becket to look out his photographic equipment, a recent hobby. Then he ordered his manservant to find him his oldest, most-worn suit, and after being helped into it, he sat down at his dressing-table and studied his face. He put pads of cotton wool inside his cheeks to plump them out and then, by dint of sabotaging a shaving brush and with a tube of spirit gum, he made himself a false moustache. Pulling an old hat down on his head, he heaved up his camera equipment and took a hackney to Brooks's and asked to see the club secretary. His voice distorted by the cotton-wool pads in his cheeks, Harry explained he was a photographer sent by the Duke of Freemount, who wanted to mount an exhibition of photographs of London clubs to show in a marquee at his annual fête. Permission was given. Harry carefully left a few bits and pieces of photographic equipment in the secretary's office.

Then, when he gratefully saw the secretary had been buttonholed by a crusty old member, he murmured something about needing more magnesium for his flash and went back to the secretary's office. He quickly searched around until he found the betting book. Quickly he scanned it and then on a page he saw that Sir Geoffrey Blandon had bet that he could obtain the favours of Lady Rose before the end of the season. Harry knew "favours" meant seduction. The bets were running at forty to one.

"Bastard," he muttered, and taking out a penknife, sliced out the page. He had meant to photograph it if he had found anything incriminating but realized it would take too long, and operating a plate camera in dim light might not produce any results at all. And the use of a magnesium flash in his office might bring the secretary running.

He went back and photographed several more of the main rooms before making his retreat.

Harry should have been happy at his success, but he wished he did not have to break such news to the earl. Lady Rose must indeed have ruined her reputation by being photographed supporting the suffragettes. She had become the subject of a common wager.

It was the day before the duke's ball when Harry Cathcart presented himself at the earl's town house.

He waited patiently in the hall while the butler took his card. While he was waiting, Lady Rose came down the stairs. She was wearing an elaborate tea-gown but her long hair was brushed down her back. Her face glowed with happiness like a lantern in the gloom of the hall. She did not acknowledge Harry because he was a stranger and she hadn't been introduced to him. Rose passed by him and disappeared through a door at the side of the hall.

Oh, dear, thought Harry. She is most definitely in love.

The butler came down the stairs and instructed Harry to follow him.

Rose picked up a book from a table in the library and made her way upstairs behind them. She wondered who the caller was. Her father was slightly deaf and his voice was loud. She was just passing the drawing-room when she heard him say, "That will be all, Brum. Leave us." As the butler reappeared and turned to close the double doors, Rose distinctly heard her father say, "Well, found out anything about Blandon?"

She stayed where she was, frozen to the spot. The butler looked at her curiously but went on down the stairs.

Rose heard the low voice of the caller and then her father's outraged shout of, "The man should be horse-whipped. My daughter's ruined." A frantic ringing of the bell was answered by a footman who leapt up the stairs, not even seeming to see Rose who stood there.

"Get her ladyship. Fetch Lady Polly," roared the earl.

Rose went into the drawing-room. "What is wrong, Pa?"

The earl held out a sheet of paper with trembling fingers. "Wait until your mother gets here."

Lady Polly, small and round like her husband, came into the room. "What is it, dear?"

"Sit down, you and Rose," said the earl, all his bluster and rage evaporating. "Bad business. Bad, bad business. Ladies, may I present Captain Cathcart?"

The captain, who had risen to his feet at Rose's entrance, bowed. "Captain, my wife, Lady Polly, and my daughter, Lady Rose. Now all sit down. Got your smelling-salts, Rose, hey?"

"I never use smelling-salts."

"You might need them now. Go ahead, Cathcart, tell them what you found out."

Feeling rather grubby, wishing he could escape and leave the earl to break the news, Harry described what he had discovered. He started by saying, "Blandon keeps a mistress in Pimlico, a girl called Maisie Lewis."

He saw the shock and dismay in Rose's eyes, followed by a defiant anger. In that moment, he knew that Rose had immediately decided that the affair with Maisie was old history.

"The affair continues," he said. "As Blandon had the appearance of a gambler, I decided to check the betting books. I thought I might find out something about financial difficulties, but instead found out that Blandon had bet that he could seduce Lady Rose before the end of the season."

The countess let out a little scream and raised a handkerchief to her lips.

The earl held out the sheet from the betting book to Rose. She read it carefully and then said, "You must excuse me. I have things to attend to."

"We can't go to the ball now!" wailed Lady Polly.

"Sir Geoffrey does not know what we now know," said Rose. "We should not give him that satisfaction."

She rose and sailed from the room, back erect, and all the love light gone from her face.

Her mother hurried after her, leaving Harry and the earl alone.

"Thank you," said the earl gruffly. "Do you mind leaving now?"

Harry rose and left the room and walked quickly down the staircase. The happiness he had felt in the success of his detective work had evaporated. He was haunted by the set, cold, bereft look in Lady Rose's eyes.

Rose entered the ballroom at the Duke of Freemount's town house the following evening, hearing the chatter of clipped voices threading through the jaunty strains of a waltz. She had artificial flowers in her hair and a white satin gown embellished with white lace and worn over silk petticoats that rustled as she walked.

She felt cold and dead. She allowed Sir Geoffrey to write his name in her dance card. He did not seem to notice any difference in her manner.

Although the ballroom was suffocatingly hot, Rose shivered in Geoffrey's arms as he swept her into the waltz. Footmen began to open the long windows which looked out over the Green Park and a pleasant breeze blew in. Geoffrey manoeuvred her toward those windows and then danced her out onto the terrace.

"I want to ask you something, my love," he whispered.

A little hope surged in Rose's heart that it had all just been a joke, that "favours" had meant her hand in marriage.

"Yes, Sir Geoffrey?"

"Tarrant's giving a house party in a fortnight's time," he whispered urgently. Through the open windows, he could see Rose's mother searching the ballroom for her daughter. "Got you an invitation. We can be together."

Rose disengaged herself from his arms and stood back a pace and faced him.

"Together? What do you mean?"

"Well, you're always chaperoned . . ."

"I would not be allowed to accept such an invitation without a chaperone."

"That's just it. I've got a friend who will pose as my aunt."

"Miss Maisie Lewis, for example?"

He turned dark red and then mumbled, "Never heard of her."

Rose turned on her heel and marched straight back into the ballroom and up to the leader of the orchestra and whispered something. He looked startled but silenced the orchestra.

Dancers stopped in mid-turn, faces turned in Rose's direction. The recently installed electric light winked on monocles and lorgnettes.

"I have a special announcement to make," she shouted. "Sir Geoffrey Blandon is a cad. He has been laying bets that he can seduce me before the end of the season. Here is the proof." She took out the page from the betting book and handed it down from the rostrum to the man nearest her. "Pass it round," she said.

Eyes stared at her in shock, so many eyes.

Then she walked down the shallow steps from the rostrum and straight up to her white-faced mother. "I have the head-ache," she said clearly. "I wish to go home."

As they stood on the steps waiting for the carriage to be brought round, the earl said dismally, "Well, that's it, my girl. I thought we'd agreed to go on as if nothing had happened. Why d'ye think I restrained myself from confronting Blandon? You're ruined."

"I? Surely it is Sir Geoffrey who is disgraced!"

"It's all right for a fellow. The chaps will think he's a bit of a rogue. When he propositioned you, you should have come straight to me. I'd have told him to lay off. But to get up there and behave like a fishwife was shocking."

Rose fought back the tears.

"Still, Captain Cathcart did the job. You'd best rusticate for a couple of seasons and then we'll try again."

TWO

✝✝

The Scotch middle or lower classes are not, as a rule, given to joking,
except with their dry, sententious humour, and they rarely understand
what is commonly called "chaff." It is better to bear this in mind, as it
may account for many an apparently surly manner or gruff reply.
—MURRAY'S *HANDBOOK FOR SCOTLAND* (1898)

Rose was only nineteen years old and, apart from her brief foray to support the suffragettes in their demonstration, had been protected from the world by loving, indulgent parents and by the sheer separation from ordinary life enjoyed by girls of her elevated class.

So she was hurt and bewildered that she should be the one disgraced and not the perfidious Sir Geoffrey. As servants packed up the belongings in the town house, preparatory to the move to the country, she hid herself in the normally little-used library and tried to find solace in books. Before her love for Geoffrey, she had damned the season as being little more than a type of auction.

But she was young, and somehow the thought that out there, beyond the stuccoed walls of the house, a whole world of enjoyment and pleasure was going on without her was galling.

She had not made friends with any of the debutantes, despising their empty chatter, and now she regretted her own arrogance.

Rose threw down her book. She would go and try to see Miss Tremp, her old governess, who now worked for the Barrington-Bruce family, whose town house was in Kensington.

She did not summon her maid but went upstairs and changed into a plain tailored walking dress and a hat with a veil.

Rose then slipped out of the house and hailed a hack. She directed the driver to the address but then realized that with her disgrace being generally known, the governess might not be allowed to see her, so instead, she lifted the trap on the roof and called to the driver to take her to Kensington Gardens instead.

It was a fine day and she knew the nannies and governesses with older charges often walked there.

She paid off the hack and began to walk slowly up towards the Round Pond, looking to left and right. Ladies in stiff silks moved along the walks as stately as galleons. Regimented flower-beds blazed with colour and a light breeze blew the jaunty sounds of a brass band to Rose's ears. The sky above was blue with little wisps of cloud. A boy bowling an iron hoop raced past her, bringing memories of childhood when one could run freely, unencumbered by corsets and bustles. Rose began to think it had been silly of her to expect just to see Miss Tremp when she spotted her quarry sitting on a bench by the pond.

Rose hurried forward and sat down next to her. "Miss Tremp!"

"My gracious. If it isnae Lady Rose!" exclaimed the governess, surprise thickening her normally well-elocuted Scottish vowels.

"I need your help," said Rose. "Where are the children?"

"Two of them, boys. They are sailing their boats in the pond, my lady, and that'll keep them busy for some time. I heard about your sad disgrace. It was in the newspapers."

Rose bent her head. The newspapers had been kept from her but she should have known she would be written up in the social columns.

"It's so unfair!" said Rose. "Sir Geoffrey should be the one in disgrace."

"Gentlemen never get the blame in such circumstances. You should know that."

"Miss Tremp, you educated me well, and for that I will be always grateful, but I could have done with a few lessons in the ways of the world."

"Listen to me, my lady, I told you I approved of the vote for women. I did not tell you to demean yourself by appearing at a demonstration. And it was up to your mother, Lady Polly, to school you in the arts of society."

Rose could feel herself becoming angry.

"It is an unfair world for women," said Miss Tremp. "But you are privileged. It is your duty to your parents to marry well and then to your husband to have his children."

"But you said women had a right to have independence and not to be a household chattel for some man!"

Miss Tremp flushed pink to the end of her long Scottish nose.

"I am sure I never said such a thing."

Rose shook her head in bewilderment. "What am I to do?"

"I think the next step is surely to send you to India. That is the procedure for young ladies who have failed at their season."

"I AM NOT GOING TO INDIA!" shouted Rose.

The nannies on either side leaned forward.

"Wheesht!" admonished Miss Tremp. "Ladies do not raise their voices."

"You are suddenly a wealth of information about what ladies do and don't do."

"You would be best, my lady, to do what your parents tell you to do. Please lower your veil. I have my position to consider."

"Do you mean you consider me a disgrace?"

"Unlike you, my lady, I have to earn my living. I was always of the opinion that you were a bit spoilt."

"Why didn't you say so?"

"It was not my place to do so."

"It was not your place to fill my head with ideas of female independence which you should surely have known I could never be allowed to follow."

"The day will come, my lady, when you will be grateful to me for a sound education to furnish your mind."

Rose stood up. She opened her mouth to deal out some final recrimination, but her shoulders sagged. She nodded her head, turned on her heel, and walked away.

She had hoped for reassurance from Miss Tremp, for comfort, for a shared outrage at the iniquities of society.

Miss Tremp watched the slim figure of Rose walking away and sniffed. That was the English for you. No backbone.

Detective Superintendent Alfred Kerridge was enjoying a pint of beer before going home to his wife, Mabel, and their two children, Albert and Daisy. He had risen steadily up the ranks by dint of diligent plodding laced with amazing flights of imagination.

He was a grey man—grey hair, grey eyes, heavy grey moustache. He felt a tug at his elbow and looked up into the unlovely features of one of his informants, Posh Cyril.

Posh Cyril was second footman in the Blessington-Bruces' household. He had a criminal record for burglary of which his employers were blissfully unaware. Although he had given up a life of crime, he had become an informant. He had been very useful in finding the identity of thieves for Kerridge, for he could recognize his own kind among the servants of various aristocratic households.

"Got something for you," he whispered.

Kerridge nodded and bought him a pint and then led the way to a corner table. They sat down. "What have you got?" asked Kerridge.

"Did you read about that scandal involving Lady Rose, daughter of the Earl of Hadshire?"

"My wife insisted on reading it out to me. Hardly a criminal matter."

"Ah, but Sir Geoffrey Blandon is being forced to leave the country."

"Shouldn't think he'd have to do that. Thought ruining some lass's reputation was fair game with that lot." Kerridge detested the upper classes with every fibre of his hard-working lower middle-class soul. He was sure one day the revolution would come. One of his rosy fantasies was a world where all the roles were reversed and the aristocrats' money would be taken from them and spread among the poor.

"It's like this." Posh Cyril leaned forward. "It was my night off and I was playing cards in the kitchen at Blandon's. The bell for the front door goes. The footman went to answer it. Then we hear shouting and swearing. I nipped up the stairs and opened the baize door a crack. There's this tall, black-haired fellow and he's smacking into Blandon with his fists. He brings him down and then he leans over him and says, 'Leave the country by tomorrow or, by God, next time I'll kill you.'"

"No charges have been laid."

"But Blandon thinks the earl hired someone to beat Blandon up. That's criminal," said Posh Cyril.

"Was the assailant some hired thug?"

"No, he spoke like a gent. Got gent's clothes on, too."

"That lot are a law unto themselves," said Kerridge. "Nothing there for me."

"The newspapers might pay for this."

Kerridge sighed. He knew if the newspapers got hold of it, he would have to investigate for the sake of formality. Then someone would have a word with someone else in high places and he would be ordered to drop it.

"Keep your mouth shut," he ordered, "or I'll make sure your employers know all about your record. Here's half a crown. Now take yourself off."

"What is it, Brum?" asked the earl the next afternoon. "Is everything ready for our departure tomorrow?"

"Yes, my lord. A person has called to see you."

"I don't see persons."

"This person is a police officer." Brum held out a small silver tray with a card on it.

The earl took it. "Detective Superintendent Alfred Kerridge. Dear me. I'd better see him. Where is he?"

"In the ante-room."

"Send him up."

Now what? wondered the earl. Have we engaged some criminal by mistake? There's that new hall boy, whatsisname.

The doors opened and Kerridge was ushered in, holding his bowler and gloves in one hand.

"Sit down," ordered the earl.

The stocky detective sat down gingerly on a delicate-looking chair which creaked alarmingly under his bulk.

"I do not want to distress you, my lord, by referring to the matter of your daughter's confrontation with a certain Sir Geoffrey Blandon—"

"Then don't."

"It has however come to my attention," pursued Kerridge, "that Sir Geoffrey was beaten up by an assailant and ordered to leave the country."

A slow smile lit up the earl's face. "By Jove! Really?"

"Yes, really. My lord, you did not by any chance hire such an assailant? My report says he spoke like a gentleman. He is tall and has black hair."

Cathcart, thought the earl, with a sudden rush of gratitude. "No," he said coldly. "I am not in the habit of hiring thugs. I should warn you. . . ."

Here it comes, thought Kerridge.

". . . that the Prime Minister is known to me."

"How did Lady Rose get that sheet from the betting book of a gentleman's club?"

"I have no idea."

"Perhaps Lady Rose could tell me?"

The earl rang the bell. "You have overstepped the mark. We have nothing to do with the assault on Blandon, and if you insist on pursuing this, I shall have a word with your superiors, not to mention . . ."

"The Prime Minister," said Kerridge.

The butler appeared. "Show Mr. Kerridge out," ordered the earl.

It was just as he expected, thought Kerridge, but perhaps his visit might persuade the earl that he was not above the law. Then he realized dismally that the earl had just persuaded him that he was.

The earl had never regarded himself a gossip and despised those whom he considered indiscreet. But when he arrived at his club an hour later and saw Brigadier Bill Handy sitting by the fire, the temptation was too much.

"Well, well," said the brigadier. "I hear you're leaving town. Bad business. Cathcart do his job?"

The earl sat down and leaned forward. "He did more than his job. Worth every penny of that thousand pounds he charged. He thrashed that bounder, Blandon, and told him to leave the country. But don't tell anyone. Most grateful to you."

"What about your daughter? There was no reason for such a scene. How could she behave so disgracefully?"

"To tell the truth," said the earl miserably, "I don't know my own daughter. She had what seemed an excellent governess. Rose wanted a good education. I should have known how dangerous that is. Men hate a woman with a brain. Not me, but then, I'm highly intelligent and sensitive."

"Quite," said the brigadier, looking with amusement at the earl's guileless face.

"When Rose took off for that demonstration, we thought she had gone off to visit the vicar. Fact was, she took a train to London. Couldn't blame the governess. She'd already left."

"What about India? Send her out there. Lots of officers. By the way, did you just say that Cathcart charged you a thousand pounds?"

"I know. I was shocked. Didn't expect the fellow to behave like a tradesman, but he did the job all right. As far as India is concerned, we'll think about that. But don't say a word about the Cathcart business."

"Wouldn't dream of it."

The next day, the brigadier was strolling along Piccadilly. He stopped to look in the window of Hatchard's bookshop. A tall, stately figure emerged. "Lady Glensheil!" said the brigadier, doffing his silk hat. Lady Glensheil was the daughter of one of his oldest friends. "How d'ye do?"

"Very well, I thank you. And you?"

"Splendid. Splendid. Oh, I say!" For a large tear had escaped from one of Lady Glensheil's eyes to cut a wet furrow through the thick powder on her cheeks.

"It's nothing," she said. Her maid stepped forward and handed her a handkerchief and she dabbed her face.

"It must be something," insisted the brigadier. "Walk a little with me and tell me about it."

He proffered his arm. She put the tips of her fingertips on it and they walked slowly along Piccadilly.

"I am ruined," said Lady Glensheil.

"Money?"

"Good heavens, no!" Lady Glensheil was shocked at the very idea that a lady would even mention such a sordid subject.

"I am here to help you," said the brigadier gallantly.

"I must talk to someone or I'll go mad," she said. "But not here." With her eyes she indicated her maid and footman following behind.

"We'll go into the Green Park," said the brigadier. "Send your servants off when we get there."

She nodded. The brigadier cast anxious little glances at her as they proceeded on their way. Lady Glensheil in his estimation was a fine figure of a woman. Others might think she had a hatchet-face but the brigadier considered it truly aristocratic. Her heavy silk gown was liberally decorated with fine lace. Her straw hat contained a whole garden of artificial flowers.

Once they reached the park, Lady Glensheil ordered her servants to walk a distance away and then sat down on a bench with the brigadier.

"Now," he said, "what do you mean, you're ruined?"

"It's simply terrible. Glensheil's up north. He detests the season. I'm here to bring Fiona out. My youngest."

"And?"

"I commissioned Freddy Hecker to do a portrait of me."

"Who is Freddy Hecker?"

"He is an up-and-coming artist. We became friendly—too friendly."

"Ah!"

"He is now blackmailing me."

"The scoundrel should be horse-whipped."

"He says unless I pay him one hundred guineas a month, he will tell Glensheil."

"Deny the whole thing!"

"I wrote him letters."

"Oh, dear."

"I don't know what to do. I feel sick!"

The brigadier sat in silence. He had promised Hadshire not to mention Cathcart. But still, he could not bear to see her suffer.

"I think I know someone who can help you. He . . . fixes delicate situations."

"Oh, please. Give me his name."

"There's only one trouble. He'll probably charge steep, about a thousand pounds."

"I have my own money. The reason I did not agree to pay Hecker was I knew he would bleed me dry."

"So it was a money problem after all."

"Certainly not. We never discuss money. You know that."

The brigadier suppressed a smile. He took out his card-case and extracted a card, wrote Captain Cathcart's name and address on the back. "That's the fellow," he said. "Go and see him but go alone."

"I don't know how I can ever thank you."

"Thank me if it works out."

"A lady to see you, sir," said the captain's manservant.

"Which lady?"

"The lady is heavily veiled and will not give me her card."

For some reason, Harry had a picture of Rose, her face illuminated with happiness—a happiness all too soon to be snuffed out.

"Send her in," he ordered.

He experienced a little pang of disappointment as the heavily veiled figure that was ushered in was obviously not that of Lady Rose. This lady had a mature figure and was dressed accordingly.

"Do sit down," said Harry. "Something to drink?"

"Nothing, I thank you."

"To what do I owe the pleasure of this visit?"

"I did not expect you to be a gentleman. I must beg you to be discreet."

"I am always discreet."

She put back her heavy veil. "I am Lady Glensheil."

She studied the captain's face but he expressed no surprise, only continued to look at her inquiringly. "Please sit down," he said, "and tell me why you have come."

She sat down opposite him and then looked nervously at the window. It was still daylight.

"Would you be so kind as to draw the curtains? Someone passing in the street might see me."

"Certainly." The captain rang a bell by his chair. "Becket," he said, when his manservant appeared, "draw the curtains and light the place."

They waited in silence while Becket drew the curtains closed and then lit the gasolier.

"That will be all," said Harry. "Now, Lady Glensheil . . ."

She opened an enormous reticule and after much fumbling produced the brigadier's card and handed it to Harry.

I may be discreet, thought Harry, but the brigadier most certainly is not.

"And what do you want me to do?"

"I am being blackmailed," said Lady Glensheil. She began to cry. Harry rang the bell again and ordered brandy. He waited patiently while Lady Glensheil's tears washed a copious amount of white lead make-up and rouge onto a delicate handkerchief. He took out a large one of his own and handed it to her.

She began to recover and even drank some brandy.

"It's all too, too terrible," she said and then regaled Harry with the story of the blackmailing artist.

"I see," said Harry when she had finished. "I suppose the first thing to do is to get the letters back."

Wild hope shone in her eyes. "You could do that?"

"I will most certainly try. I will do my best to make sure he never troubles you again."

"Oh, thank you!" Again the reticule was snapped open. This time she produced a roll of banknotes and handed them to him.

"I thought it would be more discreet to pay you in cash."

Harry hesitated. It was one thing to take cash from the earl, another to take cash from a lady in distress. But the money would set him up very comfortably. He could even rent a carriage. A proportion could go to charity to ease his conscience. "Thank you," he said. "Would you like a receipt?"

"No, please, nothing in writing. No one must hear of this."

"No one will hear a word from me. I do not go around in society much."

"I do not know why. You must come to one of my soirées."

"Too kind. But a lot of my lack of a social life is of my own choosing. Please leave this matter with me and you shall hear from me shortly. Please write down this artist, Freddy Hecker's, address."

Again the reticule was snapped open and a small notebook with a silver pencil attached produced from its depths. Lady Glensheil wrote down an address, tore off the page and handed it to him.

She rose to go. "Do you have your carriage?" asked the captain.

"Of course not. I came in a hansom."

"Then Becket will find you one to take you home. Ah, how do I contact you? You will not want me to call at your town house in case your husband is there."

"Glensheil's in Scotland. Wait, my card. Call on me as soon as you have anything." While she ferreted for her card-case, the captain rang the bell and asked Becket to fetch a cab.

Soon her majestic figure, once more veiled, had departed and there was only the faint scent of patchouli in the room and a large roll of banknotes as a reminder of her visit.

THREE

*When leaving town, it is usual to send round cards to all your friends
with the letters P.P.C (pour prendre congé) written in the corner.
This obviates the necessity of formal leavetakings.*

–FLORA KLICKMAN, *HOW TO BEHAVE*

The earl's well-sprung carriage bore them off to the country. It was a perfect day. Not a cloud in the sky. The striped blinds and awnings on the shops and houses gave the city they were leaving behind a festive air.

Rose sat in a corner of the carriage, trying to read, trying to escape from the feeling that as much as she had been tricked by Sir Geoffrey, she was as much to blame for her disgrace.

If only she had cultivated the friendship of the other debutantes, she thought again, she might have picked up useful gossip about the season in general and Sir Geoffrey in particular.

The fact was she had armoured herself in learning to combat her shy nature. She had felt her superior education had given her the edge over those other silly girls. And yet she was the one being banished from London in disgrace.

She also felt a slow burning resentment for Captain Harry Cathcart. There was no need for him to have produced such dramatic evidence to overset her. If he had not interfered, then

Geoffrey would have propositioned her and her eyes would have been opened to what kind of man he really was.

If she and the captain ever crossed paths again, she hoped she could think up some way to humiliate him.

The morning after Lady Glensheil's visit, Harry strolled along the King's Road and found a pub opposite to where the artist, Freddy Hecker, had his studio. Most of the windows were of frosted glass, but one which had been smashed recently had been replaced by plain glass.

He bought a half pint of ale and positioned himself at a table at the window and began to watch.

After an hour, a maid opened the door and handed a man his hat and stick. That must be Freddy, thought Harry.

He waited until the artist had strolled off down the road and then left the pub and went across and knocked on the door.

The maid, who was buxom and pretty, answered his knock.

"Hecker in?" asked the captain languidly.

"I am afraid the master is out, sir."

"When are you expecting him back?"

"In about an hour, sir."

"Good, I'll wait."

The maid hesitated. "Would you not like to leave your card, sir, and come back later?"

"No, my good girl, I would not. The wretched man is supposed to be painting my portrait." He loomed over her and she nervously stood aside. "Where is the studio?"

"Upstairs, sir, but—"

"I'll find my own way."

Harry went up a narrow staircase. A door on the landing was

open, revealing the studio, a vast room made up of two storeys that had been knocked into one.

"May I bring you some refreshment, sir?" said the maid's voice behind him.

"Nothing, I thank you. Run along. I must figure out which is my best side."

He closed the door behind her and began to look around. Now where would the wretched man have hidden the letters?

As he searched around behind easels propped against the wall and through boxes of materials which the artists used as back-cloths, Harry realized that this was where he worked but not where he lived.

He opened the door and went down the stairs again. The maid was waiting at the bottom.

"I've made a frightful mistake. I was supposed to call at old Freddy's home to make the arrangements. He'll be waiting there for me. Lost the address. Give it to me."

"It's at Twenty-two, Pont Street, sir. May I have your card?"

"Listen, I don't want Freddy to know I was such a chump. Don't tell him I called here first."

Harry produced a sovereign and held it up. "Promise?"

The maid took the sovereign and bobbed a curtsy. "Oh, certainly, sir. Most grateful, my lord," she added, elevating him to the peerage.

Harry hailed a hansom cab in the King's Road and directed the cabby to Pont Street. He took out a half hunter and checked the time. If Freddy had gone to his home and if he had meant that he really would be back in his studio in an hour's time, he should be leaving fairly shortly.

He strolled from Pont Street to a news vendor's kiosk and bought a copy of a newspaper. He strolled back to Pont Street, occasionally stopping to look at the paper as if he had just noticed a fascinating item. At last he was rewarded with the sight of the young artist he recognized as Freddy leaving his house. He certainly was a very handsome young man, with thick curly fair hair and a cherubic face.

The captain waited until the artist had disappeared down Pont Street. He went up to the door and rang the bell. An imposing manservant opened the door to him. Freddy must be doing well, thought Harry. The tyranny of visiting cards. He wished he had thought to have some fake ones printed.

The butler inclined his head as Harry cheerfully presented his own card and said he had just met Mr. Hecker in Pont Street and Mr. Hecker had told him to wait for him.

He was led upstairs to a drawing-room on the first floor. Harry refused refreshment and said he would sit and read his paper. When the butler had left, he looked around. The furniture and ornaments were expensive. Harry wondered for the first time if Lady Glensheil was the only victim of the artist's blackmailing.

There was no desk in the drawing-room. He reflected that if there was a study it would possibly be on the ground floor.

He cautiously eased out of the drawing-room and stood on the landing. The house was silent. He went quietly and swiftly down the stairs and listened again. A murmur of voices came up from the basement. He opened doors until he found a study and went over to the desk by the window. He opened drawer after drawer. The bottom left-hand drawer was locked.

He took out a sturdy Swiss knife and selecting the tool designed for taking stones out of horses' hooves, prised the drawer open. There were bundles of letters. He took them all out, deciding not to risk looking through them in case he was caught. Harry looked around for something to carry them in and finally put them all in a wastepaper basket, then went out to the street door and, after lifting his visiting card from the tray in the hall, let himself out.

When he had reached the safety of his own home, he went through the letters and put them into neat piles on his desk. Apart from the ones from Lady Glensheil, there were letters from six other members of society.

He wrote down the six names and asked Becket to find him their addresses, and when his manservant returned with the information, he set out. First he called on Lady Glensheil, who cried this time with gratitude, and then he tracked down the six others, making sure each time to see them on their own and without their husbands. It seemed unfair that the six should get his services for nothing whereas Lady Glensheil had to pay, but he was afraid that if he asked for money, they would assume he was a blackmailer as well.

When he returned to his home in the evening, it was to find a furious artist on his doorstep. Hecker's manservant had remembered Harry's name. "I am bringing the police into this," shouted Hecker. "You broke into my desk and stole my property."

"I must say you have a bloody nerve," said the captain. "Let's both go to Scotland Yard, now. Of course it will come out that you are a blackmailer and you will be ruined."

Hecker's bluster left him. "No need for that. But I warn you—"

"No, I will warn *you*. All the money you blackmailed out of these ladies must be discreetly returned, every penny. In a few days' time, I will check to see if you have done so. It would give me great pleasure to ruin you, but in doing so I would ruin your victims' reputations as well." He leaned forward on the doorstep and smiled into Hecker's face. "If you do not do what I say, I will shoot you."

"You can't do that!" Hecker turned pale. "This is England."

"Marvellous country, isn't it? Now, stop fouling my doorstep and make a noise like a hoop and bowl off." Harry put his hand on the artist's face and shoved and sent Hecker flying down the steps to land on the pavement.

Harry let himself in with his key. He doubted that he would hear from Hecker again.

High summer spread across the English countryside. Society moved out to Biarritz and Deauville, returning in August for grouse shooting in Scotland. Lady Rose read, walked through the countryside, and sometimes thought she might die from boredom and loneliness.

As August moved into September, the earl received a visit from Baron Dryfield, who owned one of the neighbouring estates. The little earl was glad to receive him. Because of Rose's disgrace, he felt ostracized from local society. The baron was a huge jovial man, a great favourite of King Edward's.

"I need to talk to you privately," said the baron. Lady Polly, who was in the drawing-room with her husband, rose to her feet and left the room.

"What is it?" asked the earl, alarmed. "What is it that my wife can't hear?"

"You will shortly hear from the palace that His Majesty is going to favour you with a visit in September."

"But that's wonderful news. It means the scandal is buried. Great expense, of course."

"Well, the bad news is there's a buzz at court that our king wants to try his luck with Rose. She's become a sort of challenge, see. They call her The Ice Queen."

"What am I to do?" wailed the earl. "How can I protect Rose? If he asks, say, to go for a walk with her, I can hardly refuse."

"Bless me, I don't know. But thought I'd warn you."

Captain Harry Cathcart had been busy all summer. Word had got around, and in a society rife with scandal, his services were in demand. There was nothing very dramatic, mostly petty business which could be solved with shrewd advice, but his bank balance was getting fat and he now had a carriage and pair.

He found to his surprise that he was also much in demand socially. His taciturn manner, damned before as boring, was now considered Byronic. But he accepted few invitations. His experiences in the war seemed to have left a dark, sour patch inside him.

One morning he received an urgent telegram from the Earl of Hadshire, asking him to travel to the earl's home, Stacey Court, as soon as possible.

The captain packed a suitcase and set out with his man, Becket. They took a hack to Paddington Station and the Great Western Railway train to Oxford, planning to take the local train at Oxford, which would bear them on to Stacey Magna, the nearest station to the earl's home, where they would be met.

Harry was unusual in that he had bought first-class train tickets for himself and Becket. Normally the master travelled first class and the servant in the third-class carriages at the back of the train.

Half-way to Oxford, Becket fell gently asleep and Harry studied his servant's face. After his discharge from the army,

Harry had taken to walking around the streets of London to exercise his injured leg. One morning early he had been in Covent Garden market, watching the porters carry in great baskets of vegetables when one of them collapsed and sent the contents of the basket of potatoes he had been carrying spilling across the cobbles.

"Bleedin' milksop," jeered one porter. "Leave him lie, Bert. Ain't nuthin' but a shyster."

Harry had picked Becket up and supported him into a nearby pub and had bought him a brandy. Then, realizing by the man's emaciated form that he was starving, had ordered him breakfast. Becket had fallen on the food, shovelling it desperately into his mouth.

"I've been hungry like that," thought Harry with compassion, a picture of lying under the hot sun on the African veld swimming into his mind.

When the man had finished eating, Harry questioned him. Becket, too, had been a soldier, and having left the army, found it hard to get work. He had a thin, sensitive white face, straight brown hair combed severely back, pale grey eyes and a thin mouth. He said he'd been in the army since he was a boy but would offer no further clue to his background.

On impulse, Harry explained that he, too, had recently returned from the wars and was on a small budget, but if Becket liked to follow him home, he would find work for him.

And so Becket had fallen into the role of manservant. He could read and write and studied books on how to be the perfect gentleman's gentleman. He only spoke when spoken to, never complained, even when his wages were late.

As Harry did not like people asking him questions, particularly about the Boer War, he respected his servant's reticence.

Although Becket was expected to eat the same food as his

master, he was still thin and pale, but apart from that seemed healthy and strong enough.

Harry, resplendent in new morning dress and silk hat, arrived finally at Stacey Magna, to be met by the earl's coachman and two footmen who bore them off in a well-sprung carriage to Stacey Court.

Stacey Court was a Tudor mansion, built of red brick and with many mullioned windows which flashed and twinkled in the summer sun as the carriage bowled up a long drive under an avenue of lime trees. Harry was surprised to think of Lady Rose in such an antique setting. He had pictured her in a stately Georgian home with portico at the front and long Palladian windows.

Brum, the butler, was on the steps to meet them. Two footmen followed the butler with the luggage up an old oak staircase and then along a corridor which seemed to be full of steps up and steps down and threatening overhead beams, in places so low that the captain had to duck his head.

The room Harry was ushered into had a magnificent four-poster bed. A small adjoining room had been allocated to Becket. Somehow Harry was glad that his manservant was to be close at hand and not confined to the servants' quarters, although Becket would be expected to take his meals in the servants' hall. Harry was told the earl expected him in his study as soon as he had freshened up after the journey. There was a spot of soot on his shirt-front. Becket changed him into a clean shirt and bent down and gave his master's shoes a polish.

"What will you do?" asked Harry after he had rung the bell to be conducted to the earl's study.

"I will go down to the servants' hall, sir."

"Get on all right, will you? I mean, you haven't been with other servants before."

"I am sure I shall manage."

Harry looked at him doubtfully, wondering how his manservant would cope with the rigid class system that existed among servants in large houses.

A footman appeared and Harry followed him along the corridor and then back down the stairs under the gaze of family portraits to the hall, where Brum was waiting to take over. He led Harry across the hall and into the study on the ground floor.

"There you are again," said the earl gloomily. "I'm in a fix. Sit down. Have sherry. Help yourself. Have you eaten?"

"I had lunch on the train. Let's get to business."

"Right. His Majesty is threatening to come on a visit."

"A great expense."

"That's not the problem. It's Rose. I've heard a whisper that His Majesty is going to try his luck with her."

"And you want the visit stopped?"

"But how?"

"Leave it to me."

The earl and Lady Polly had intended to keep the news of the captain a secret, but Rose was accompanied on her walks by her maid and a footman. Two days after the captain's visit, as she was walking along a country lane, she was only dimly aware of the footman, John, and her maid, Yardley, talking in low voices. But she heard the name "Cathcart" and swung round.

"What about Cathcart?" she demanded.

"I was saying that we did not often get callers," said Yardley, "and John here was remarking that the last caller was a certain Captain Cathcart."

"Back to the house," ordered Rose and set off at a great pace.

She marched into her father's study as soon as she arrived

home. The earl was asleep in an armchair by the window, a newspaper over his face. Rose snatched the newspaper away and shouted, "Pa! Wake up!"

"Eh, what?" The earl struggled awake and looked up into the furious face of his daughter.

"What was that man doing here?"

"What man?"

"Cathcart."

"Oh, him. Just a social call."

"I don't believe it."

"Don't you dare to question me, my girl! I told him to call if he was ever in the neighbourhood and he did, and that's that. Now run along."

After a few days, as Rose was being dressed for dinner by Yardley, she heard a carriage arriving and went to the window and looked down. Her mouth tightened into a thin line. Captain Harry Cathcart descended and then helped a woman down from the carriage. He held out his arm to her and they disappeared below the window up the stairs to the main door.

"Hurry up!" snapped Rose to her maid. "We have visitors."

She waited impatiently while the maid finished strapping her into a long corset and putting on her stockings and attaching them to the long suspenders. Then came the knickers, several petticoats and a taffeta evening gown. Her hair was then pulled up over the pompadours, or rats, as the pads were commonly called, and pinned in place. Rose snatched up her evening gloves and put them on as she headed rapidly out of the room.

She made her way down to the drawing-room to find only her mother there. "Dinner has been delayed a little," said Lady Polly. "You father has business to attend to."

"What business?"

"I am afraid I do not know. I never interfere in your father's business affairs."

"It's something to do with me. I know it." Rose paced up and down.

"The world does not revolve around you," said the countess sententiously. "Do sit down."

But Rose continued to pace.

The doors were thrown open and the earl appeared, followed by Harry and a cheaply dressed over-made-up girl. She was wearing a tight gown of lavender crêpe de Chine. The neckline was very low and the gown appeared to be held up by two strings of beads on the shoulders. Her hair was an improbable shade of gold. Rose thought she must have travelled in evening dress, for there had surely been no time for such a quick change.

"Captain Cathcart, you know," said the earl. "May I present Miss Daisy Levine."

"Pleased, I'm sure," said Daisy, sinking down into a low curtsy. Her face was covered in white lead with two rouged circles on her cheeks and her long eyelashes were darkened with lampblack. Her large green eyes were slightly protruding.

Lady Polly stared at her husband with a look of outrage on her face.

"I've told Brum to lay two more places for dinner," said the earl. "We've got fifteen minutes. I wanted to keep this from you, Rose, but the captain says that for reasons of security you must be told, and all the servants as well."

Rose sank down into the nearest chair, her legs suddenly weak. From the look of amazement of her mother's face, she realized it was a mystery to her as well.

"Perhaps you will explain, Captain," said the earl.

The captain courteously helped Miss Devine into a chair and then sat down himself.

"His Majesty plans to come here on a visit," he began.

"But that's wonderful!" cried Lady Polly. "It means our dear Rose is re-established."

"I am afraid not," said Harry. "It appears His Majesty means to try his luck with Lady Rose."

There was a stunned silence, finally broken by a giggle from Daisy. "Wish he'd try me. I'd be set up for life."

"He must be put off coming but in such a way as not to offend him," Harry went on. "Miss Levine is an actress. She will play the part of a servant who has contracted typhoid."

"Is that necessary?" asked Rose, finding her voice at last. "Could we not just tell him one of our servants has the typhoid?"

"I think someone from the royal household will be sent here to confirm the fact. We must be prepared for that. A telegram will be sent off tomorrow."

"The servants will all need to be told of the subterfuge," said Rose. "Would it not have been easier to pretend to hire Miss Devine? Then she could have pretended to have contracted typhoid. In that way, none of our servants would need to know."

"Miss Levine will be excellent in the part of someone dying of typhoid," said Harry. "I doubt if she would last a day as a servant without being dismissed. Besides, there is not time to find her fake references."

"I'm ever such a good actress," mumbled Daisy, beginning to be intimidated by the glacial stare the countess was turning on her.

"Dinner is served," intoned Brum from the doorway.

The earl and countess went first. Harry offered his arm to Rose. She ignored him and walked alone after her parents, so he offered his arm instead to Daisy.

Dinner was a nightmare for Rose. She hated Harry. She was sure he must be mistaken.

The earl was a kindly man, so he courteously asked Daisy about her theatrical career. Daisy, warmed by wine and attention, revealed she was a Gibson girl, one of that famous chorus line. She told several funny stories and the earl and Harry laughed appreciatively while Rose and her mother picked at their food.

When Lady Polly finally rose as a signal to the ladies to follow her to the drawing-room, Rose pleaded a headache and retired to her room.

She allowed Yardley to help her out of her dress and to unlace her corset and then dismissed her, saying she would cope with the rest herself. Rose found these days that she craved solitude. She had begun to slip out in the evening after everyone had retired, climb down the tree outside her window and go for a walk in the garden, so that when she did finally go to bed, she would be tired enough not to lie awake, playing her humiliation over and over in her head.

When the house was finally silent, she put on a divided skirt and jacket, opened the window and began to climb down.

Harry's room afforded a good view of the moonlight-bathed rose garden underneath. He saw a dark figure slip across the rose garden and disappear through an arch at the end.

He left his room and went down the staircase. He did not want to go through the process of unlocking the great front door, which had been bolted and locked for the night, so he went into the earl's study, opened a window and stepped out onto the terrace.

He silently made his way round the house to the back where the rose garden lay and walked across it and then through the arch at the end.

He found himself in a knot garden, laid out in the original Tudor lines, the low box hedges protecting the flower-beds.

The moon had gone behind the clouds and he could dimly make out a figure seated on a stone bench.

He went quietly forward. The moon slid out from behind the clouds again and he found himself looking down at Rose. Her head was bent and he wondered whether she was crying.

He was about to quietly retreat when she looked up and saw him. "Why are you following me?" she asked harshly.

"I saw a figure in the gardens and decided to investigate. Are you distressed because of His Majesty's proposed visit?"

"Of course. Please go away. I hate you."

"But why? Would you rather Blandon had seduced you?"

"If you had left things alone, he would have propositioned me, I would have refused, and that would have been that."

"But he did, I gather, and you refused, and yet you made a scene and brought the whole matter to the attention of society!"

She gave a pathetic little shrug. "What do I care? The season is a farce. I am better off without a husband. Now, please leave me in peace."

Harry bowed and walked off. He felt angry. Ungrateful little minx!

A telegram was sent off the next morning informing the king of the servant's illness. Daisy was confined to a servant's room in the west wing.

Despite her distaste for the whole business, Rose found herself becoming curious about the girl. In the first place, to be a Gibson girl at the Gaiety Theatre meant beauty and elegance. Rose had seen postcards of the Gibson girls on sale in the village shop.

Her curiosity got the better of her and one morning she called on Daisy. The chorus girl was lying listlessly in bed, staring at the ceiling.

"I brought you some books and magazines," said Rose. "You must get very bored."

Daisy yawned and stretched. Without her make-up, she seemed little more than a child. She made an effort to get out of bed, but Rose held up one hand. "As we are all in this deception, there is no need to rise for me. Have a look at these books. I do not read much fiction, but there are a few novels there."

Daisy sat up in bed and took up one of the novels. "Looks all right," she said, after apparently scanning a page.

"You are holding the book upside down," said Rose quietly. "You cannot read or write, can you?"

"No, my lady," said Daisy, hanging her head.

"And you are not a Gibson girl either, are you?"

Daisy mournfully shook her head from side to side. "I asked the captain to let me say I was, this place being so grand. He got me from Butler's." Rose looked puzzled. "It's a vaudeville place down the East End. Ever so rough, it is."

Rose drew up a chair to the side of the bed, the light of a crusader in her eyes. "If you wish, I can teach you to read and write. You could better yourself. Come along. Think of it. It would pass the days. There is no need for you to lie here. We could use my old schoolroom."

"Anythink's better than this, my lady."

"I will wait outside the door until you are dressed," said Rose firmly.

King Edward was unusual in that he enjoyed being king. He was not given to either introspection or abstract ideas. Perhaps for that reason, he became easily bored. He was seated at the Duchess of Freemount's dinner table and the duchess recognized with alarm the danger signals coming from the king. His heavy eyelids were falling, his voice was deepening and slowing up and his podgy fingers were drumming on the arm of his chair.

"I believe you are not going to the Hadshires' after all," said the duchess.

"Some servant girl's got typhoid. Whole place in quarantine."

"Indeed! Poor Lady Rose must be feeling very bored. Banished from society and then quarantined. Your visit would have restored her. Such a beauty. I am surprised they did not rush the wretched servant to some hospital, fumigate the place, and then go ahead and entertain you."

A spark of interest lit the king's eyes. He studied the duchess for a long moment and then said, "Think Hadshire's faking it?"

"I never said that, sire." The duchess twinkled at him and gave him a knowing little smile.

The lessons in the schoolroom were interrupted two days later when a footman burst into the room and shouted, "Sir Andrew Fairchild, for the king. He's here!"

Rose and Daisy rushed back to the west wing. Rose helped Daisy out of her clothes and into a nightgown. Daisy quickly applied a white lead cosmetic to her face. "I don't think we need to worry," whispered Rose. "He will not dare risk infection. But if he comes, play your part well."

She shot out of the room, and hearing footsteps ascending the staircase, dived into another servant's room and stood with her ear against the door.

She heard her father protesting, "I'll never forgive myself if you catch this awful infection."

They went on past where she was hiding. "In here," she heard her father say. "If you don't mind, Sir Andrew, I'll wait downstairs. The footman will bring you back when you're ready."

Rose waited until her father had left and eased out into the corridor. John, the footman, saw her and Rose held a finger to her lips for silence. They both stood listening.

They heard Daisy say in a weak voice, "The angels are coming for me. I hears the beating of their wings. Is that a light in the sky? Is that you, Mother?"

Oh, Lord, thought Rose bitterly. She's overdoing it. She put a handkerchief over her face and walked past the footman and into the room. "There, now, dear girl," she said firmly. "You must not tire yourself by talking. Sleep now." She flashed a warning look at Daisy, who subsided into silence.

"Come away, Sir Andrew," ordered Rose. "It is dangerous to be so close to the infection."

"Doesn't seem to bother you, hey?"

"It is my Christian duty to do what I can," said Rose firmly. "Your arm, sir."

He reluctantly held out his arm and Rose took it and urged him back along the corridor.

———

A week later, the earl was informed by telegram that the king would be visiting him in a month's time. "I'll send that wretched girl packing. It's her fault the trick didn't work," raged the earl, erupting into the schoolroom.

"A word with you outside, Pa, if you please."

Father and daughter walked outside and down the corridor a little way. "Pa," said Rose firmly, "I do not wish Daisy to leave until I have taught her how to read and write."

"Stuff and nonsense. Didn't do you much good, did it?"

"I beg you to let her stay. I have nothing else to occupy my time. Unless, of course, I do some work for the suffragette movement."

"Don't you dare!" yelled the earl. "Oh, keep your latest toy. I'm wiring Cathcart."

FOUR

✠

*As a rule, the men-servants in large houses expect gold. These
gratuities are really a great tax on people's purses; and the question
whether to accept an invitation is often decided in the negative by the
thought of the expenses entailed, not by railway tickets and cabs, but by
the men and the maids.*

–LADY COLIN CAMPBELL,

ETIQUETTE OF GOOD SOCIETY (1911)

"I wonder why our king got suspicious," said Harry to his man-servant after reading the earl's telegram.

"Perhaps one of his servants talked."

"He assured me they were all very loyal."

"A royal visit would mean a great deal of money in tips for the servants, not to mention the prestige of having served His Majesty. They may have felt balked and bitter that such a visit was cancelled."

"We'd better deal with it, anyway. Know anything about dynamite, Becket?"

"Nothing, sir."

"Where would I find out?"

"I read somewhere, sir, that they were blasting a new railway tunnel on the underground railway at Liverpool Street Station.

Perhaps one of the workers there might be able to supply you with some dynamite and instructions as to how to use it, if discreetly bribed."

"Good man, Becket."

Harry, disguised in clothes purchased at a second-hand clothes store, made his way late in the afternoon to Liverpool Street Station. He located the site of the new tunnel, located the gate where the workers would come out and waited patiently. At seven o'clock, dirty, weary men began to file out. Leaning against a hoarding, Harry studied their faces. He at last picked out a man older than the rest. His face was criss-crossed with broken veins and his nose was bulbous, all the signs of a heavy drinker. He followed him as he walked from the station, keeping a steady pace behind him. He was feeling decidedly weary as he trudged along, his bad leg aching, wondering if the man lived at the ends of the earth, but his quarry finally opened the doors of a pub in Limehouse and walked in. Harry gave it a few minutes and then walked in as well.

The air was full of the smell of pipe smoke and cheap cigarette smoke. The smoke lay in wreaths across the dingy pub, which was lit by flickering gas lamps.

The smell of unwashed bodies struck him like a blow in the face. He went to the bar and ordered a pint of porter and looked around. The man he was chasing was carrying a full pint to a corner table. Harry picked up his drink, walked over and sat down.

"I want to talk to you," he said.

"What about?" The man took a pull at his beer. "Who are you?" he growled. An evil-looking prostitute with sagging breasts and black teeth leaned against Harry's shoulder. "Fancy a good time, guv?"

"Shove off," said Harry.

He waited until she had gone.

"My name's Bill Sykes," said Harry.

"Bin reading Dickens, 'ave you?" sneered his companion.

Harry cursed himself. He should have guessed that a dipsomaniac, like many of his kind, would turn out to have come down in the world.

"My mother did," said Harry. "Your name?"

"Pat Brian."

"Mr. Brian, I have an offer for you. How would you like to earn two hundred guineas?"

"Garn."

"The truth."

"What d'ye want for it?"

"A quantity of dynamite, enough to blow up, say, a bridge and a building, and instructions on how to do it."

"How did you know I was a blaster? Come on. Who's bin talking?"

"No one. Lucky guess." I am a rank amateur, thought Harry. He could have turned out just to be one of the labourers.

"Two hundred guineas. What's it for?"

"The two hundred guineas are for you to supply the material and instructions, keep your mouth shut and not ask questions."

"Two hundred guineas!" Pat stared into his beer and then took a long pull. "I could quit. I could get back to Ireland. Buy a bit o' land, I could."

"When could you get the stuff?"

Pat finished his drink. "Come along o' me. Going back to Liverpool Street."

"Have you a key to the site?"

"Don't need one, guv. Know a way in. How do I know you'll pay?"

Harry slid a wash-leather bag out of his pocket and passed it over. "Look in there. Under the table."

Pat fumbled with the bag under the table. His eyes widened. He stuffed the bag in his jacket pocket. "Thanks," he jeered. "You'd best walk out of here. One shout from me that you're the perlice, and they'll murder you."

Harry sighed. He fished in his other pocket and then said levelly, "I now have a pistol pointed at your private parts under the table. Give me back the gold or I'll blow your manhood off."

Pat ducked his head under the table and then straightened up. He shrugged. "Worth a try. Can't blame me, now can you, guv?"

"Get to your feet and walk to the door. I will follow. You now know too much, so if you attempt to run away, I will shoot you."

"You're going to force me to get the stuff for nothink," wailed Pat, his accent an odd mixture of Irish and Cockney. "Jesus, Mary and Joseph. I have no luck at all, at all."

"You'll get your money. Now, walk!"

"That person is here again," complained Rose.

"If you mean Captain Cathcart, yes," growled her father. "And speaking of persons, why hasn't that Daisy creature been sent packing?"

"I am teaching her to read and write, Pa. When she has mastered both, she will find a good position, possibly as a clerk, in London. I would like a typewriter."

There were two reasons why the earl finally capitulated and gave in to his daughter's demands. Rose kept busy with her protégée was less likely to get into trouble, and a typewriter was considered to be a woman's machine and was designed with scrolls of gold on black to give the machine the feminine touch.

Rose went immediately to find the earl's secretary, Matthew Jarvis, to instruct him to order a typewriter and have it delivered as soon as possible. Matthew nodded and said he would attend to the matter immediately. Matthew was a chubby man whose clothes always seemed too tight for him. He had a round red face, a heavy moustache, and little brown eyes.

Daisy had been regaling Rose with stories of her sometimes quite horrific childhood in the East End of London. Rose had begun to wonder about people in the household, realizing they had lives and thoughts of which she had hitherto known nothing.

"Are you happy here, Mr. Jarvis?" Rose asked.

"Yes, my lady."

"You have worked for my father for five years now. Do you sometimes find the job a little tedious?"

Matthew looked shocked. "Not in the slightest, my lady."

"Your family, do you visit them?"

"Yes, my lady. If you will excuse me, I will continue with my work. I will now be able to telephone to order the typewriter, my lord having recently had that very useful instrument installed."

"Very good. Oh, Mr. Jarvis?"

"My lady?"

"I believe Captain Cathcart is with us, but so far I have not seen him. Where is he?"

"To my knowledge, he is working in a downstairs room in the east wing."

"At what?"

"I am afraid I could not say."

Curiosity sent Rose on a search of the east wing. It had been added on to the main Tudor building in the days of Queen Anne. It was usually where the guests were housed when the earl and countess held a party.

She found the captain in a little-used room at the end of a corridor on the ground floor.

"Don't you ever knock?" he asked angrily, when she walked in on him.

"You forget. This is my home. I have no need to knock. I see you have a quantity of sticks of dynamite. Are you going to blow up the king?"

"No, I am going to create a couple of explosions. I have already written several anonymous letters to the newspapers warning them of a Bolshevik plot against the king."

"The Bolsheviks do not advocate terrorism. It was in their manifesto."

"Didn't stop them killing Tsar Alexander the Second."

"That was the last century. That was the Nihilists. The Bolsheviks have eschewed terrorism in their new manifesto."

"Well, according to me, they haven't. Now, if there is nothing else . . ."

"Just one thing. You should wear gloves."

"I did not know there was a drawing-room etiquette to deal with dynamite."

"You must be careful of sweating."

"My dear goose, I am as cool as cucumber sandwiches."

"I didn't mean you. I mean the dynamite. Sweating is a problem with nitro-glycerine material. If it gets absorbed through your skin, you will get a nitro-glycerine headache."

Harry, who had been kneeling on the floor, beside the cases of dynamite and percussion caps, rose to his feet. "Has it never occurred to you, Lady Rose, that your knowledge is unwomanly?"

"Not in the least. I see you are as stupid and old-fashioned as the other men in society. You would feel more comfortable were my conversation limited to discussion of the latest Nell Gwyn hat, the Camille Clifford coiffure, the Billie Burke shoes and the Trilby overcoat. Good day to you."

I hope she never marries, thought Harry savagely, or her husband will wring her neck. But he put on a pair of gloves.

He decided to go for a walk in the afternoon. The sound of voices came from the paddock at the back of the stables. He walked over and leaned on the fence. Rose was giving Daisy riding lessons. At first he did not recognize the chorus girl. Her face was free of paint and she was wearing a chic riding outfit which Rose had ordered for her from John Barker of Kensington for the princely sum of one hundred and five shillings. It had a tightly cut bodice, lightly boned to the waist, and the skirt was cut to accommodate the right knee when mounting side-saddle. Over the bodice went a very tight waistcoat.

"That's right," Rose was saying. "Stand on the mounting block. Oh, I nearly forgot. You must unbutton your waistcoat first. Never mount when buttoned up or the buttons will pop and fly all over the place."

Daisy put a foot in the stirrup, grasped the pommel, heaved herself up and went straight over the other side. Rose gave an exclamation of dismay.

She rushed to help Daisy up and then both girls burst out laughing. Harry moved away, puzzled. What on earth was that little chorus girl doing with Lady Rose?

Up until that day, he had dined separately in the quarters he had set up in the east wing. He decided it was time he joined the family, and when he returned to the house he sent a note by a footman to say he would be pleased to join the earl and his family for dinner that evening.

Because of Rose's disgrace, he expected there to be only himself as a guest. But the little earl was popular and had lately found courage to send out a few invitations. There were three guests other than Harry: the Marquess and Marchioness of Hedley, the rector, Mr. Busy, and a faded cousin of Lady Polly's.

The marquess was a jovial man who liked to model himself on King Edward. He was heavy-set and heavy-bearded. His marchioness was a timid, crushed lady, as if her spirit had been borne down by her husband's relentless joviality.

Rose, reflected Harry, was looking exceptionally beautiful in a white chiffon gown and with white silk roses in her hair. He wondered how Daisy fared in the rigid snobbish hierarchy of the servants' hall.

He tried to engage Lady Hedley, who was seated on his right, in conversation. "The weather has been very fine this summer," volunteered the captain.

"Yes, indeed," she said. "Strawberries were fine. Yes." Then she relapsed into silence.

"Lady Rose appears to be in full bloom tonight," pursued Harry.

"Yes. Fine. Pity."

"Pity?"

"All that beauty. Spinster. Can't be anything else now."

"Society has a short memory."

"Not that short," she said gloomily. She cast a sudden waspish glance in her husband's direction and muttered, "Men with beards shouldn't eat soup. Disgusting."

There seemed to be nothing to reply to that, so Harry turned his attention to the pale cousin on his other side. What was her name? Ah, Miss Durwant-Flint.

"Do you live far away, Miss Durwant-Flint?"

"London."

"Ah, where in London?"

"What's it to you?"

"I was just making conversation," said Harry.

"I don't like conversing during dinner. No one should have to converse while they are eating. Barbarous."

Harry gave up and finished his dinner in silence, which took quite a long time because there were eight courses. At last Lady Polly rose and the ladies followed her out. The gentlemen were left alone with the port.

Mr. Busy, the rector, had fallen asleep. His mouth was open. He should have been called Mr. Lazy, thought Harry.

Hedley told several smoking-room anecdotes and laughed immoderately at his own humour. Then he fixed his bloodshot eyes on Harry. "Don't say much, do you?"

"Don't get much chance," said Harry coldly.

"You're a young man. You should try to be more *cheery*," said Hedley, relishing the sound of the latest slang word. "Wait a bit. You're that chap who fixes things."

The earl looked at Harry and shook his head to convey the message that he had not been indiscreet.

Harry found he had conceived a strong dislike for Hedley, so he smiled enigmatically and said nothing.

"I asked you a question," said Hedley.

Harry smiled and poured himself another glass of port. "And I didn't answer," he said.

Hedley gave him a baffled stare and then turned his attention to the earl. "Seems a shame you should all be in purdah because of little Rose. I'm giving a house party in a month's time. Got a few eligibles coming. Young people. Send Rose."

"That's very kind of you," said the earl. "I am sure my wife will be free to chaperone her."

"Don't need a chaperone. Her maid will do. M'wife'll look after her."

"Well, I suppose . . ."

"Just the thing she needs."

"Oh, all right, then."

What's going on here? wondered Harry. Does this jovial marquess really want to do Rose a favour?

The village of Stacey Magna was one of those places that look so well portrayed on chocolate boxes and were uncomfortable to live in, the thatched cottages being damp and insanitary. The inhabitants lived a quiet rural life, but were saved from the misery of poverty which plagued other agricultural villages in England, for the earl was a generous landlord and made sure everyone had enough food and that there was a school for the children.

Two evenings later, the inhabitants went to bed soon after the sun had set, to save the expense of candles, and a deep quiet settled over the houses and the surrounding countryside.

But they were all awakened at midnight by a tremendous explosion. The braver ones rushed out to see what had happened; the others cowered in their beds thinking the Day of Judgement was at hand.

It transpired that just before the main entrance to the earl's estate, where a pretty hump-backed bridge spanned a river, the whole bridge had been blown up. Just as several men from the village were exclaiming over the smoking ruin, there was another huge explosion, bigger this time, from the direction of the railway.

They set off in that direction, keeping together, looking fearfully to left and right. When they reached Stacey Magna Station, the smoke was just clearing. Great holes had been blasted in the platforms on either side and the railway line was a twisted wreck.

The blasts were too late to feature in the morning newspapers, but they hit the headlines the day after. The press arrived but were kept firmly outside the gates of the earl's estate. Crowds of sightseers came to see the destruction wrought by the Bolsheviks. And, of course, it must have been the Bolsheviks, for all the papers said so, and all claimed to have received anonymous threatening letters. Police combed through the debris and Detective Superintendent Alfred Kerridge was on his way to supervise the search.

The visitors brought some prosperity to the village, where lemonade stands and pie stands were set up, and the small pub, the Stacey Arms, did a roaring trade.

In all the fuss, Harry and his manservant, Becket, travelled in one of the earl's carriages to a railway station farther up the line and caught a train to London from there.

"Glad that's over," said Harry. "I thought I might blow myself up by mistake. I never want to handle dynamite again."

"If I may venture an opinion, sir."

"By all means."

"I was surprised you went to such lengths."

"I had to make sure the palace thought it the work of the Bolsheviks. Anything less, and they might have suspected Lord Hadshire of getting up to tricks. The palace sent a telegram just before we left, cancelling the king's visit 'for reasons of national security.' By the way, I was amazed to see Daisy Levine still in residence. Lady Rose appears to have made a pet of her. Does she eat with the servants?"

"Yes, sir."

"They must make life difficult for her."

"On the contrary, sir, Miss Levine is somewhat of a pet in the servants' hall as well."

"How did she manage that?"

"She sings very prettily and delighted the servants with impersonations of Miss Marie Lloyd."

"Indeed! I trust they treated you well, Becket?"

"At first they were hoity-toity, you not being considered a gentleman."

"Good heavens! Why not?"

"You are employed by the earl, therefore you work, therefore you are not a gentleman. But thanks to Miss Levine, I became popular."

"How did you manage that?"

"I play the concertina, sir. I accompanied Miss Levine. The butler, Brum, declared we were both so talented, we should be on stage at the Gaiety Theatre."

"Amazing. I have never heard you play, Becket."

"I did not wish to disturb you."

"Disturb me now. Got the instrument with you?"

"Yes, sir. That round box on the rack."

"It's a wonder you didn't sell it when you were so poor."

"I bought another when you paid me my back wages."

"Let's hear a tune."

Becket lifted the box down and took out the concertina. He sat down and began to play "Goodbye Dolly." Harry leaned back, the Boer War song bringing painful memories. "Play something else," he said harshly.

Becket began to play "Down at the Old Bull and Bush" while the train rocked and swayed on its way to London.

———

At Stacey Court, Brum opened the doors of the drawing-room and intoned in a voice of doom, "Detective Superintendent Kerridge, my lord."

"Come in. Sit down," said the earl. "Something to drink?"

"No, I thank you, my lord. This gentleman with me is Detective Inspector Judd. He will take notes."

Judd, a tall thin man with a black drooping moustache, carefully placed his bowler hat on a side table and took out a large notebook.

"Apart from yourself and the countess," began Kerridge, "who else was there?"

"About twenty-five indoor servants."

"I'll get to them later, with your permission. Did you have guests?"

"Just my wife's cousin, Miss Durwant-Flint, and Lord and Lady Hedley."

"Anyone else?"

"Let me think." The earl screwed up his face like a baby about to cry. Then his face cleared. There was no harm in mentioning the captain's name. It would mean nothing to Kerridge.

"Oh, yes, nearly forgot. Captain Harry Cathcart."

"And is the gentleman still in residence?"

"No, he's tootled off to London."

"May I trouble you for his address?"

The earl tugged at a bell-rope by the fireplace, and when a footman appeared asked for his secretary to be sent to him. Matthew appeared. "Get Cathcart's address for the superintendent," ordered the earl.

"I may have lost it," said Matthew cautiously.

"No, you haven't," said the earl, and winked furiously.

"Quite right, I haven't," said Matthew. "I'll fetch it now."

What was that all about? wondered Kerridge. He continued the interrogation but the earl said he had been asleep at the time, and as the bridge and station were miles from the house, he hadn't heard a thing.

Later, Kerridge did not get any further with the servants, thanks, he thought, to the perpetual presence of Brum. He got only one thing. A little scullery maid said that the king was to come on a visit but couldn't now and Brum had snapped at her and sent her from the room.

Kerridge wondered about the king's proposed visit all the way back to London. Certainly a visit from King Edward, who would arrive with a retinue of servants, guests and hangers-on could mean a crippling amount of money to the unfortunate host, but the earl's home and his estates showed no signs of penny-pinching. He shook his grey head. To think that the earl would blow up a railway station and a bridge just to put the king off was ridiculous. All Bolshevik sympathizers in London were being rounded up and interrogated. Still, he'd better see this Captain Cathcart and find out what he had to say.

The first motorized taxi cabs were beginning to appear on the streets of London and were regarded with suspicion by most, who preferred the horse-drawn variety. But as Kerridge was driven in the new Scotland Yard police car to Captain Cathcart's address, he felt like a king. He wished he could take this splendid vehicle home to show his wife.

He had decided to interview the captain alone. He knew people were often intimidated by the sight of a policeman or a detective in the background, taking notes.

At the house in Water Street, Becket announced him and led

him into the front room, where the captain was sitting at a desk at the window.

Kerridge's first impression of the captain was that he was a dangerous man. His brooding saturnine good looks gave the impression of action and power.

Harry welcomed the superintendent and then sat staring at him vacantly.

"I have come about the bombing of Stacey Magna," began Kerridge.

"Frightful, what," commented Harry. He took out a monocle, fixed it in one eye and stared at the detective.

"Yes, it was indeed frightful. Now—"

"Caught any of these Bolshevik chappies yet?"

"No, sir, but we will . . . provided it turns out to be the work of the Bolsheviks. Have you known the Earl of Hadshire for long?"

"Don't know. People come and go." Harry let the monocle drop and fixed the detective with a vacuous stare.

"His Majesty was supposed to visit Lord Hadshire, but the visit had to be cancelled."

"Pity."

"Have you any reason to suppose the earl did not wish this visit?"

Harry laughed, an insolent braying laugh. Then he said, "I say, you think old Hadshire crept out during the night and blew up things to keep kingie away?"

"It is a flight of fancy, I admit," said Kerridge. "Let's take it further. The earl employed someone to blow up the bridge and the station."

Harry grinned. "Go on. I'm enjoying this."

"It is not a laughing matter, sir," said Kerridge severely. "It was just fortunate that there was no one on the bridge at the time or in the station."

"True, true," said Harry. "Ask me some more questions."

"During your stay at Stacey Court, did you see any suspicious people lurking around?"

"Only that cousin of Lady Polly's. What a bore! I nearly fainted in my soup."

"So you can tell me nothing to help me?"

"I'm afraid not."

"What was the reason for your visit?"

Harry glared at him. "My dear sir, one goes into the country on many visits to many households. It's what one does."

"I forgot, sir. Of course it is what one does when one does not have to work for a living."

"Oh, we aren't all lilies of the field, y'know. Viscount Hinton has been wheeling a piano-organette around the streets these many years."

"But he doesn't have to. He's eccentric."

"What about the House of Lords?"

"What about it?" jeered Kerridge. "Waste of time, if you ask me. Half the house is absent and the other half's nearly dead."

"Dear me, Super, you're quite the little Bolshevik yourself."

"I beg your pardon, sir." Kerridge was shocked at his own behaviour. If his injudicious remarks got back to Scotland Yard, he would lose his job. He plodded on with the questioning, reflecting as he did so that the captain was one of the most empty-headed men he had met.

But when he got back to his desk at Scotland Yard, he turned over his conversation with the captain. He had an obscure feeling that he had somehow been irritated and manipulated into betraying his radical views. And then, there had been that odd business of the earl winking at his secretary.

That evening, before going home, he dropped in at the pub in the hope that Posh Cyril might be around, but there was no sign of the footman. He took his leave and bumped into Posh Cyril in the street outside.

"I want a word with you," muttered the superintendent.

"Walk away and into the alley along there. Be with you in a mo', " whispered the footman. "Got a friend in the pub and don't want to be seen with you."

Kerridge stood impatiently in the alley amongst the dustbins until the footman appeared.

"I need some information," said Kerridge. "I want to know about a certain Captain Harry Cathcart. Lives in Water Street, Chelsea."

"I'll find out what I can. Cost you."

"Always does," said Kerridge gloomily.

Shortly before Rose was due to visit the Marquess of Hedley, her maid, Yardley, gave notice. Lady's maids prided themselves on the appearance of their employers. Yardley felt her position in life had diminished through Rose's disgrace. Rose did dress for dinner, but during the day went around in skirts and shirt blouses, or in riding dress.

Lady Polly felt her daughter was going too far when Rose calmly announced that Daisy would be her new lady's maid.

"That girl is out of the gutter," raged Lady Polly.

"Daisy is bright and intelligent and a quick learner," said Rose. "You never talk to her. I will fetch her and you can see for yourself."

Lady Polly was taken aback when Daisy entered the room. The blonde hair was beginning to grow out and Daisy was dressed neatly and becomingly.

"So you think you can be a lady's maid?" demanded the countess.

"Yes, my lady. I have learned a great deal, thanks to Lady Rose's kindness."

Her voice was soft, with only the slightest Cockney edge.

"I do not like to think of a girl of your background chaperoning my daughter," said Lady Polly, who had the staccato speech of her class, an icy stare put into words.

"A girl of my background is wise to the ways of men, my lady. I would have protected Lady Rose better had I been with her in London."

"And do you know how to sew?"

"Yes, my lady. I worked as a seamstress in Whitechapel when I wasn't on the boards."

The countess's own lady's maid, Humphrey, stood behind her mistress's chair, darting jealous looks at Daisy. She gave a little cough. "May I suggest a test, my lady? Your blonde straw hat needs retrimming. I suggest it is given to this person to see how she can work."

"Excellent. Fetch it here and give it to the girl."

Two days later, the refurbished hat was presented to the countess. It was decorated by beautifully made scarlet silk roses. The countess was immensely pleased with it. But Humphrey snorted and said dresses were another thing. What about my lady's ballgown, which had a torn hem, and that my lady had said was old-fashioned?

The dress was returned in another two days. The neckline had been slightly lowered and the shoulders decorated with white silk bows. The train had gone and it was now ankle-length.

"I always have a train," complained the countess.

"Trains are going out of fashion, my lady," said Daisy demurely. "I could not help noticing that you have very fine ankles, and if you adopt the new style, you will not need to throw the train over your arm when you are dancing or risk it being torn when you are walking about."

The countess poked her ankles out from beneath the gown and studied them complacently. "Very good, Daisy. But you cannot be called Daisy and you cannot be called Levine because it sounds foreign. You will be called Baxter."

"That means you can go," said Rose when Daisy told her. "But I shall not call you Baxter.

"I have made an enemy of Humphrey," said Daisy. "What if she finds out you did all the sewing yourself?"

"There is no need for her to find out. We have been spending too much time over our books and typing lessons, Daisy. Now you must learn the ways of the lady's maid. When we get to Hedley's, you will dine with the housekeeper. Your behaviour must be precise. I allow you too much laxity. While we are at the Hedleys', you never sit down in my presence or wear a hat in the house. You do not venture an opinion, unless asked for it. And you never even say 'Good morning' or 'Good night.' We have a little time to bring you up to the mark.

"I prefer to dress and undress myself now that Yardley is leaving. But this you must never tell a soul or I shall be damned as middle-class. The lady's maid I had before Yardley left a notebook. I shall find it for you. In it she has written all the recipes for cleaning clothes, hats and shoes. The wash for my hair is quite simple. One pennyworth of borax, half a pint of olive oil and a pint of boiling water."

She studied Daisy for a moment and then asked, "Do you not find your life here dull?"

"Oh, no, my lady. I like dull. I can't get enough of dull. And three good meals a day!"

"Very well, Daisy. There is one thing more. I have over-prided myself on my intelligence but I lack common sense. I made a bad mistake with Blandon."

"I'll tip you off if there's another masher," said Daisy eagerly. "Can tell 'em a mile off."

FIVE

O blind your eyes and break your heart and hack your hand away,
And lose your love and shave your head; but do not go to stay
At the little place in What'sitsname where folks are rich and clever;
The golden and the goodly house, where things grow worse for ever;
There are things you need not know of, though you live and die in vain,
There are souls more sick of pleasure than you are sick of pain

–G. K. CHESTERTON, *THE ARISTOCRAT*

Rose began to feel apprehensive as her father's coach bowled along the country roads towards Telby Castle, home of the Marquess of Hedley. Would the other guests shun her? If they do, she thought fiercely, then Daisy and I will simply pack up and go home. There had been no need to buy new clothes for the visit. Lady Polly had pointed out to her daughter that a fortune had already been spent on dresses for the season.

The sky was a clear hard blue and there was a chill in the air. The leaves on the trees were blazing with autumn colours.

A new beginning, thought Rose. Perhaps this is a new beginning. And if not, well, there were jobs in London for women who knew how to type. There were lodging houses for businesswomen at reasonable rates. Whatever happened, she was resolved not to rot in the country for the rest of her life.

She was wearing one of the new corselets which had very slight boning, and had left off the usual padding. She had covered her gown with a heavy cloak before making her goodbyes to her mother, knowing that Lady Polly would have been appalled to learn that her daughter was not steel-corseted into the fashionable hourglass figure and leaning-forward look.

Under her tailored travelling dress she was wearing a silk petticoat with a frou-frou of ruffles from the knee to the hem. Rose, who had considered her mind above fripperies, nonetheless enjoyed the swishing rustling sound the petticoat made when she moved.

Daisy was learning to be a lady's maid very quickly, but Rose often sensed a naughtiness in her little maid and often wondered how long Daisy would be content to be a servant.

Telby Castle had been built in the latter years of the old queen's reign. It was a sort of folly with towers and battlements, arrow slits and stained-glass windows. It even had a drawbridge and a moat.

The new building had replaced a Georgian gem of a house with furniture and rooms designed by Robert Adam.

"Not a good master," volunteered Daisy, who had been told she was allowed to speak freely when she was alone with her mistress.

"Why do you say that?" asked Rose.

"Didn't you notice? When we came through Telby Village, it was ever so poor."

Rose had been brought up like everyone else in England to believe that God put one in one's appointed position, but surely not to abuse that position, she thought, wondering if she might find the courage to tell the marquess he ought to do something about his tenants. Then she sighed. Such a remark would be considered the height of unfeminine insolence.

She was shown to an apartment in one of the four towers. To her relief, Daisy was allocated a small room off her own bedchamber. When the housekeeper left, Rose said, "When you go down to the servants' hall, you will need to find out which is my bell. Oh, there's the dressing gong. I wonder who else is of the house party."

Daisy was rapidly unpacking the trunks. "What dress, my lady?"

"White, I suppose. The moiré with the lace inserts. My pearls, I think. White gloves. The kid shoes with the little bows and those new sequinned evening stockings."

Daisy helped Rose put her hair up over the pads and fixed it in place after she had dressed. "You look really beautiful, my lady. Maybe there's a handsome gentleman in the party."

"After my recent experience, I have no interest in men."

"Garn!"

"No, I mean it. Now pick up my stole and fan and follow me to the drawing-room. The second gong has just been sounded. You'd better ring the bell first and get a guide."

A liveried footmen escorted them down from the tower into an enormous fake baronial hall where fake suits of armour glistened under fake tattered medieval flags.

A butler took over and led them across the hall, opened a heavy carved door and sonorously announced, "Lady Rose Summer."

It seemed to Rose at first that she had entered a room full of staring eyes. Red light from a large fire flickered on monocles and lorgnettes. Then the marchioness came forward. "Nice to see you, dear. Pleasant journey?"

"Yes. I—"

"Good. Let me see. Take you round. Introductions. No, I won't. You'll get to know everybody in good time. Ah, dinner."

"Got the honour," said a young man with patent-leather hair, holding out his arm. "I'm Freddy Pomfret. Deuced fine place this, what?"

"Very fine, yes," said Rose politely and was led into dinner. She wondered briefly whether the marquess would serve roast ox to chime with the surroundings, but the dinner was the usual extravagant fare. A large silver epergne in the centre of the table depicting General Wolfe's army scaling the heights of Quebec restricted her view of the guests opposite her. Freddy was on her right and his friend, Tristram Baker-Willis, was on her left.

The words of Miss Tremp came back to Rose. "Ninety men out of every hundred," the governess had said, "offer a remark upon the weather, but unless there has been something very extraordinary going on in the meteorological line, it is better to avoid the subject if possible."

Fortunately for Rose, the bomb explosions near her home fascinated her two dinner companions so much that she was obliged to say little. Freddy ranted about the Bolsheviks and when she eventually turned away to Tristram, he ranted in much the same vein.

At last the marchioness rose as a signal that the ladies were to follow her to the drawing-room.

Rose had counted nine men and nine women in the house party, the number not including their hosts.

The marchioness introduced Rose and she tried to remember all the names. There were two American sisters, Harriet and Deborah Peterson, buxom and healthy-looking but disappointing Rose because they did not have American accents but the clipped, staccato speech of the others.

Then there was a thin, waspish girl called Mary Gore-Desmond who said little but kept flashing angry little resentful glances all around her. A Scottish beauty, Frederica Sutherland, was telling them all about the joys of hunting in a voice which could have been heard across two six-acre fields and three spinneys.

Mrs. Jerry Trumpington, ensconced in an armchair by the fire, was a toad of a woman with a fat lascivious face and very thick lips. She was talking about food to a dark, elegant woman, Margaret Bryce-Cuddlestone.

Standing together in a corner: mousy Maisie Chatterton, and a tall, pseudo-theatrical lady called Lady Sarah Trenton.

After the introductions, it looked as if Rose was going to be ignored, but Margaret Bryce-Cuddlestone approached her and said with a smile, "Are you getting over your terrible treatment at the hands of that cad, Blandon?"

"I'm getting over it," said Rose ruefully, "but I don't think anyone else is."

"Walk with me a little," urged Margaret. "That awful Trumpington woman is about to heave herself to her feet. She's just been watching you as if you are a particularly succulent lamb chop. If we engage in deep conversation, she'll hopefully leave us alone. This party does seem like a bore and I've only just arrived. Still, we've all got to find husbands."

"Have you had a season?" asked Rose.

"Yes, and I failed. Ma and Pa got two offers for my hand and I turned both down, so I'm in disgrace. I was let out of my cage to go to this house party and more or less ordered to come back with a husband."

"Is there anyone you find attractive? Who are they all?"

"Well, there're your dinner companions, Freddy and Tristram. Need I say more? The Honourable Clive Fraser is handsome and rich, but dull, very dull. Sir Gerald Burke is terribly amusing. Quite the rattle. But no money and there are rumours that he was, well, a friend of Oscar Wilde."

"Is he a playwright as well?"

"Not quite. Harry Trenton is so-so—hunts, shoots and kills everything that moves, ideal for the Scottish female over there. Jerry Trumpington is married to the awful Mrs. Trumpington. And then there is Neddie Fremantle. He's called Neddie because he laughs like a donkey, haw, haw, haw. And finally Bertram Brookes, quiet and acidulous."

"It was very kind of Lord Hedley to invite me," said Rose. "As you will understand, I have not been in the way of getting any invitations at all."

"It'll pass. You are not what I expected. The rumour was you didn't like anyone and talked like an encyclopaedia."

"I wanted to find an intelligent husband," mourned Rose.

Margaret gave an elegant little shrug. "You will have to forget that. They do not exist in our class. Did you not meet young men before your come-out? There must have been the local hunt balls and parties, dinners and so on."

"My parents really thought I was a schoolgirl and I am afraid my governess did not remind them of my age. It was only on my seventeenth birthday when they asked how old I was that they realized they would need to prepare me for a season. So I was trained in etiquette and dancing by various ladies. I first attended a few parties, just before the start of the season in London, but it was at one of those parties that I met Sir Geoffrey."

Margaret nodded in understanding. Parents of their class quite often saw little of their children.

They were then joined by the gentlemen. Freddy and Tristram bore down on Rose and began to pay her extravagant compliments until she felt she couldn't bear their company any longer. She excused herself and went to her hostess and pleaded she had a headache. The marchioness summoned Daisy, and, followed by her maid, Rose escaped.

Once in her room, she confided in Daisy. "I had to get away. There were two young men praising my appearance in a very *warm* way which I felt was not at all the thing."

"Who were they?" asked Daisy, taking the bone pins out of Rose's hair.

"Freddy Pomfret and Tristram Baker-Willis."

"What do they look like?"

"In a way, almost alike. They both have short dark hair smeared down with grease and very white faces and rather thick white lips. Both very slim. Freddy has a small moustache and Tristram is clean-shaven. It's all right, Daisy, you can go to bed. If you just help me out of my gown and unfasten my stays, I can do the rest."

Daisy lifted the gown over Rose's head and then untied the ribbons of the corselet.

"I really do feel a fish out of water," mourned Rose as Daisy stooped and unclipped the long suspenders. "But there's something odd about this house party. Or maybe it is just me and there's nothing odd at all."

"Never mind, my lady. It's the first day. Would you like me to fetch you a cup of Bournville cocoa?"

"That would be very welcome. Press the bell."

"It's all right, my lady. I'll go to the kitchens myself. Got to find my way around."

Daisy left and went down the stairs. Once in the hall, she could hear one of the ladies singing in a high reedy voice while someone accompanied her on the piano.

She went straight to the dark recesseses at the back of the hall and pushed open a green baize door.

Down the winding stone staircase and into the vast kitchen, where plates of sandwiches were being piled up. "Not more food, surely," said Daisy. The butler looked across at her in surprise. "Our guests always have sandwiches before they go to bed."

"I came to get a cup of cocoa for my lady," said Daisy.

"I'll fix it for you," grumbled the cook.

"Just give me the tin and show me where the milk is and I'll do it myself," said Daisy.

The butler, Curzon, had heavy eyebrows and they nearly disappeared under his hairline. "You are lady's maid to Lady Rose Summer, are you not?"

"Yes."

"And you are?"

"Daisy Levine."

"Levine, I suggest in future you remember your place. You should have rung the bell."

"Now I'm here, I may as well get it," said Daisy pertly.

"Oh, let her get it," snapped the cook. "We're all exhausted."

She took down a tin of Bournville cocoa and placed it with a jug of milk on the table, along with a small pan.

"Ta," said Daisy.

Curzon headed off out of the kitchen, followed by three footmen carrying trays of drinks and sandwiches.

"You got on the wrong side of him," said the cook.

"Don't care. Don't live here, thank God," said Daisy. "You'd think they'd have built a modern house instead of this castle."

"It's not bad. There's a lot of help and the stove's gas. The last place I worked they hadn't changed anything in the kitchen since the eighteenth century. And gaslight everywhere here. No need for oil lamps."

"Some houses in London have electricity," said Daisy.

"I'm Mrs. Mason," volunteered the cook. "Your young lady got herself a bit of a reputation."

"Wasn't her fault," said Daisy.

"Lady Rose should be careful. Some of these young men like to roam the corridors when they've had too much to drink."

Daisy carefully measured cocoa into a cup, lifted the pan from the stove, and carefully filled a cup.

"Thanks," said Daisy, heading for the door.

"Ring the bell next time," said Mrs. Mason. "Old Curzon is a stickler for etiquette."

Daisy made her way rapidly back up to the tower. But when she entered Rose's room, it was to find her mistress was fast asleep. Daisy turned off the gaslight and sat down in a corner and sipped the cocoa.

It would be the way of the world, she thought, if Rose were regarded as some sort of fallen woman. Men never got the blame. She finished the cocoa and went out again and listened. The guests were beginning to retire for the night. Daisy sat and waited and waited. It might be as well to take precautions.

"Jolly useful having cards on the doors," whispered Freddy to Tristram an hour later. The bed candle he was holding dripped hot wax on his hand and he swore. All the gaslight had been turned off for the night.

"I say," said Tristram, staggering and holding on to the wall for support, "we won't go too far, will we?"

"Bit of a kiss and a cuddle. Say she asked us to call. With her reputation, who's going to believe her?" Freddy giggled and hiccupped. "Hold the candle up so as I can read the card on the door. I thought this was her room."

"No, it's that old fright, Mrs. Jerry Trumpington. Try the one below."

They staggered together back down the staircase. "Here, let's try this door," said Freddy. "Ah, got it. Here we go."

He opened the door gently and they both approached the bed on which a silent figure lay asleep.

Freddy lay down on one side of the figure and Tristram on the other.

"Now," whispered Freddy. He grabbed the sleeping figure.

Which shot up and screamed and screamed. A shaft of moonlight fell on the terrified features of Mrs. Jerry Trumpington.

"Sorry," babbled Freddy. "Thought it was my room."

Mrs. Trumpington's lady's maid rushed in and began to scream as well. Sir Gerald Burke appeared in the doorway. Freddy and Tristram tried to get past him but he blocked the way. More guests began to appear carrying bed candles.

Daisy joined the crowd. When all attention was focused on the guilty pair, she slid Rose's card neatly out of the holder and put back Mrs. Trumpington's card.

"What is going on here?" demanded the Lord Hedley.

"Frightfully sorry, wrong room," pleaded Freddy.

But Mrs. Trumpington had recovered from her fright. As her maid lit the gaslight, a distinctly salacious look began to appear in her small eyes.

"Two of you got into my bed. Why was that?"

"Too much to drink," said Tristram desperately.

"Oh, you naughty, naughty boys," said Mrs. Trumpington.

"What's the matter?" Mr. Trumpington, a small man with a beaten air, shuffled to the front of the crowd wrapped in a violently coloured silk dressing-gown.

Mrs. Trumpington laughed. "I do believe these wicked, wicked boys were trying to seduce me."

"Can't be true," said her husband. "I mean, why?"

"Downstairs, you two," said the marquess to Freddy and Tristram. "The rest of you go to bed."

Daisy slipped quietly back up to Rose's room. Rose was fast asleep. She had not awakened during the whole commotion.

Rose entered the breakfast room the following morning still blissfully unaware of the happenings of the night before. One long sideboard was laden with a row of silver dishes kept hot by spirit lamps. There was a choice of poached or scrambled eggs, bacon, ham, sausages, devilled kidneys, haddock and kedgeree. An even larger sideboard offered pressed beef, ham, tongue, galantines, cold roast pheasant, grouse, partridge and ptarmigan. A side table was heaped with fruit: melons, peaches, nectarines and raspberries. And in case anyone should prove to be still hungry—scones and toast and marmalade and honey and specially imported jams.

Rose, an early riser, was relieved to see there was only one other guest in the breakfast room, Margaret Bryce-Cuddlestone.

"You look very bright and fresh," commented Margaret. "Never tell me you slept through the whole thing."

"What whole thing?"

So Margaret told her. "This is outrageous," exclaimed Rose when she had finished. "I'd better go home."

"These things happen. No one else will mention it to you and the two culprits will never dare even approach you again. It is my belief that someone took the card from your door and put it on Mrs. Trumpington's door. Mr. Pomfret and Tristram Baker-Willis were so fuddled with drink that they had lost their minds."

Rose still looked distressed, so Margaret said, "Just think of it. The awful Mrs. Trumpington remains convinced it was her favours they were after."

Rose began to laugh. "That's better," said Margaret. "Let's go for a walk after breakfast."

"I suppose I'd better get Daisy to accompany me."

"Daisy?"

"My lady's maid."

"You call her Daisy?"

"Her surname is Levine and my mother wanted me to re-name her Baxter, but I didn't like that so I compromise by using her Christian name."

"Yes, bring her along. I call mine by her first name. She is Colette Bougier and she complained that the English servants called her Booger. As she is a very good lady's maid I capitulated and now I call her Colette."

The castle gardens lay outside the walls. The lady's maids walked behind their mistresses, who had both changed into walking clothes after breakfast.

Colette put her hand on Daisy's arm, causing her to stop until Margaret and Rose had moved out of earshot. "Terrible last night, was it not?" she whispered. "The way they do go on. In France one keeps the mistress discreetly hidden."

"My lady is nobody's mistress," said Daisy hotly.

"I did not mean that. I mean, they say they put the cards on the bedroom doors so everyone can know which is their room, yes?"

"Yes, surely—"

"No, it is because perhaps some gentleman is protected from making the dreadful mistake of sleeping with his wife instead of his mistress."

"You mean they ain't got no morals," said Daisy and quickly corrected herself, ever mindful of Rose's teaching. "They haven't any morals?"

"Only the young ladies go on as if they are in the convent."

"Going to be a dull party, then," said Daisy cheerfully. "Mostly young ladies."

"Ah, but even they can fall. I know . . ."

"Colette! My shawl," called Margaret, "And do keep up with us."

Colette ran forward and wrapped the Paisley shawl she had been carrying around her mistress's shoulders.

Rose had been telling Margaret all about Sir Geoffrey Blandon and how her father had hired a certain Captain Cathcart to find out about him.

"I've heard a rumour about a certain captain who fixes things, covers up scandals, things like that. What's he like?"

"Nothing out of the common way," said Rose stiffly. "Quite rude, in fact."

"Has he done any more work for your father?"

Rose longed to tell her new friend all about the king's aborted visit but decided that it was something she could *never* talk about. "No, and I hope I never see Captain Cathcart again."

The house party settled down to a routine of shooting and hunting for the men in the afternoons while the ladies read or sewed or played croquet. Then, after another long boring dinner, there were charades or cards. Rose found the company of Sir Gerald Burke amusing and her new friendship with Margaret enjoyable and yet she longed to go home.

There was an atmosphere in the castle she did not like. Almost at times a feeling of menace.

And yet the marquess paid her a great deal of fatherly attention. Finding out she liked to read, he took her on a tour of his library, proudly showing off leather-bound books bought by the yard from the bookseller, with little attention to content.

The weather had turned dark and stormy and the folly of having arrow slits in the walls of the towers was soon revealed as the wind screeched through them like so many banshees.

One particularly vile night, Rose sat up in bed reading a novel by H. G. Wells, unable to sleep because of the noise of the wind. Draughts were everywhere, seeping through the windows and under the doors, causing the flames of the candles to flicker.

And then she thought she heard a voice calling, "Fetch the doctor."

She got out of bed just as Daisy came into the room. "I heard something, my lady. Did you hear it?"

"It sounded like someone calling for a doctor. I hope nothing has happened to Miss Bryce-Cuddlestone. Pass me my dressing-gown, Daisy."

"I'm coming with you," said Daisy.

Wrapped in dressing-gowns, they opened the door. There were faint sounds coming from downstairs on the left.

They went down the stairs, the light from their bed candles throwing up great shadows on the stone walls. Then there was a scream.

"I think it's from the other tower. It's along this corridor here," whispered Daisy.

They made their way along the long corridor which connected the towers. Lady Hedley appeared from a room at the end of the corridor. Her face was chalk-white and she had a handkerchief pressed to her lips.

"Go back to your room, Lady Rose," she said. "We are waiting for the doctor. Miss Gore-Desmond is . . . has been . . . is ill."

But other guests appeared behind Rose and they all clustered forward despite the marchioness's protests.

The gaslight was flaring in Mary Gore-Desmond's room. Rose had a brief glimpse of a still figure on the bed, the marquess, the butler, the housekeeper, and Mr. Jerry Trumpington, when the marquess turned round and with his face red with anger shouted at them to go away.

"I wonder if they'll manage to get a doctor on a night like this," whispered Daisy. "I think she's dead."

SIX

✠

We are at the cross-ways. If we stand on in the old happy-go-lucky way,
the richer classes ever growing in wealth and in number, and ever
declining in responsibility, the very poor remaining plunged or plunging
even deeper into helpless, hopeless misery, then I think there is nothing
before us but savage strife between class and class.

–WINSTON CHURCHILL, SPEECH AT LEICESTER, 1909

"Daisy! What are you doing?"

Rose had just come down to the main hall on her way to
breakfast the following morning to find Daisy standing with her
ear pressed against the door of the earl's study.

"Sorry," said Daisy, darting guiltily away from the door and
joining her mistress. "But it's ever so interesting."

"Don't say 'ever so,'" Rose corrected automatically. "You
should not listen at doors. It's vulgar."

"Lord Hedley is in a right rage. Seems it's not the usual
doctor but a new one, the old one having popped his clogs last
week."

"Daisy!"

"And he won't sign the death certificate!"

Now Daisy had Rose's full attention. "Why not?"

"Seems like this new doctor, a Dr. Perriman, well, he says

it's arsenic poisoning, of that he's sure. Lord Hedley, he says, 'So what?' He says a lot of ladies take arsenic to clear the skin and she's overdone it. Dr. Perriman says he's already phoned the police and Lord Hedley is raging and saying he'll have him drummed out of the medical profession."

There was a thunderous knocking at the door and both women jumped nervously.

The hall-boy, who had been slumbering in a chair near the door, awoke with a start and rushed to open it.

A police sergeant stood there, with a constable at his side. The butler, Curzon, appeared in the hall.

The police sergeant said something in a low voice and then both policemen were led off to the study.

The castle was hushed and sombre. The wind had died down but great black clouds still tore across the sky.

Rose was once more on her way downstairs for afternoon tea when she heard Curzon announcing in tones of doom, "Detective Superintendent Kerridge."

The superintendent and another detective vanished into the marquess's study. Rose joined Margaret and the others in the drawing-room where a lavish afternoon tea was being served.

The American twins, Harriet and Deborah Peterson, were whispering together. The rest were moodily silent until Mrs. Trumpington raised her voice. "Who just arrived? I heard a carriage. Curzon?"

The butler, who had entered the room after Rose, said, "Persons from Scotland Yard have arrived, madam."

"Oh, this is ridiculous." Mrs. Trumpington selected a large slice of Madeira cake, scoffed it down, brushed off the crumbs which decorated her jet-embroidered gown, and declared, "I mean, the silly girl obviously took arsenic for her skin. Took too much, that's all. And anyway, that doctor had no right to jump to the conclusion that it was poisoning. And how does he even know it was arsenic?"

"He says she smelled of garlic," said Sir Gerald-Burke.

"So?"

"Evidently a sign of arsenic poisoning. Then she'd vomited all over the place and—"

"Ladies present. I say." Harry Trenton.

"You did ask," remarked Gerald languidly. "It's all such a bore. I suppose we will all have to be interviewed by the police."

Lady Sarah Trenton gasped and fell back in her chair with her eyes closed.

"Has she fainted?" asked Neddie Freemantle.

"Acting as usual," said Frederica Sutherland roundly. "She's always acting and posing."

Sarah opened her eyes and glared at them all. "I have delicate sensibilities which the rest of you seem to lack."

"Did they find arsenic in her room among her cosmetics?" asked Margaret.

"I don't know," said Mrs. Trumpington. "Ask the maids. There's been an army of them in there cleaning up and laying her out."

"That's destroying evidence," gasped Rose.

They all stared at her and she flushed at being suddenly the centre of so much attention. "It's just that Scotland Yard has recently opened a fingerprint bureau. If the room had not been cleaned, they could have taken all our fingerprints and discovered if there was anyone who had been in her room."

"Trust our walking encyclopaedia to know that," said Gerald waspishly, and Rose, who had begun to regard him as a friend, gave him a hurt look.

The door opened and Lord Hedley came in. "The police want to interview you one at a time. Sorry about this. It's all the fault of that doctor, Perriman. First it's the working classes getting uppity, now it's the middle classes. They make trouble to get their revenge on us."

"Why would they want to do that?" asked Rose.

"Envy. Pure envy," said the marquess. "Your parents phoned, young lady. I told them there was no need to travel here. Once this trivial matter has been resolved, we can all relax and enjoy ourselves. Now, the police will begin with the ladies. Lady Rose? Perhaps you should go first."

"Why?" Rose wanted to ask. But she got up and followed the marquess through a door in the hall and along a corridor. "I've put him in the estate office," said the marquess. He ushered Rose in and closed the door.

Rose and Kerridge took stock of each other. Kerridge saw a very beautiful girl in high-boned white lace blouse and tailored skirt. Rose saw a thickset grey-haired man, with calm grey eyes and a thick grey moustache, standing behind a desk.

"Please be seated, my lady," said Kerridge. Another detective sat a little away from Kerridge and a policeman with a large notebook was perched on a hard chair in a corner of the room. A stuffed fox glared down from the wall behind the desk, its mouth open in a snarl.

"Now, Lady Rose," said Kerridge, "where were you on the night Miss Gore-Desmond died?"

"I was in my room and I heard someone shouting—I think shouting, 'Get a doctor.' My maid and I put on our dressing-gowns and followed the sound of the voices. Lady Hedley came out of what I now know to have been Miss Gore-Desmond's room. She said Miss Gore-Desmond had been taken ill. I had a glimpse inside the room of Lord Hedley, the butler and housekeeper, and, I think, Mr. Trumpington. I am afraid that is all I can tell you."

"What kind of lady was Miss Gore-Desmond?"

"I didn't really get to know her. She seemed—well, prickly, as if she despised us all."

"Did she favour any gentleman in particular?"

"Not that I noticed. She sewed a lot. Petit point. She did not converse much, or if she did, I did not notice. Will that be all?"

"Just one other thing. Do you know a certain Captain Harry Cathcart?"

High colour stained Rose's cheeks. "I believe he is an acquaintance of my father."

"The bridge and the station at Stacey Magna were blown up."

"Yes, but what has that to do with the death of Miss Gore-Desmond?"

"Just curious. Have you any idea who was responsible?"

"The Bolsheviks, of course. Everyone knows that."

Rose thought she heard him mutter, "Except me," but could not be sure.

"That will be all for now. Shall I ring for a footman?"

"I can find my own way back, thank you."

He consulted a list. "Would you be so kind as to ask the Misses Harriet and Deborah Peterson to step along?"

"Certainly."

"Why did you ask her about that business at Stacey Magna?" asked Inspector Judd.

"Because I have a nagging feeling that it had more to do with stopping the king visiting than any plot by Bolsheviks. But we'd better stick to this business here. What's worrying you, Judd? You've a face like a fiddle."

"You say this Lord Hedley is rich."

"Yes, very."

"And yet you say those suits of armour are fake? Why didn't he have real ones?"

"No feel for history. I was reading up on this place. There used to be a beautiful house here and Lord Hedley's father tore it down and took out all the Adam furniture and burnt it all. He built this about thirty years ago, when everyone wanted everything to look like something out of the Knights of the Round Table."

The American sisters entered the room and Kerridge began to question them. After they had left he worked his way through all the guests, ending up with the Marchioness of Hedley.

"Are you going to be long?" she asked.

"No, my lady," said Kerridge soothingly. "Just a few questions."

"No. Meant are you going to be long *here*? Tiresome. Can't abide policemen."

"This may be a case of murder," said Kerridge severely.

"Tish, tosh! Silly girl used the stuff as a cosmetic. That's all."

"Did she have any enemies?" pursued Kerridge doggedly.

"Well, nobody liked her. I didn't."

"Why, my lady?"

"Why what?"

"Why did you not like her?"

"No grace. No manners. Ferrety little thing."

"Why did you invite her?"

"Hedley's idea. 'We'll have a season's-failures party.' That's what he said."

"But the Misses Peterson, the Americans, have not yet had a season?"

"Them? They're foreigners. Need all the help they can get."

"Was Miss Gore-Desmond romantically involved with any of the gentleman?"

"Not that I noticed. My husband will speak to your superiors. And the—"

"Prime Minister," Kerridge finished for her.

"Him, too. Now bustle along. Silly doctor. Not one of us."

After she had left, Kerridge heaved a sigh. "Better start on the servants. I hear someone arriving." He walked to the window and looked down into the courtyard. A smart new motor car had just pulled up. Getting out of it was a tall man accompanied by a servant.

Kerridge rang the bell and waited until a footman appeared. "Who is the new arrival?" he asked.

"I believe a Captain Harry Cathcart has arrived, sir."

"Indeed," said the superintendent thoughtfully. "Now I wonder what he's doing here."

"Where are you to be lodged?" the captain asked his manservant.

"With all the valets and lady's maids, accommodation is limited. I am to share a room with Freddy Pomfret's valet."

"Find out what the servants are saying about this mysterious death."

"Of course."

"I'm uneasy about this one," said Harry. "Hedley wants me to fix things so that it will appear as an accidental death. But I don't see myself covering up for a murder."

"I will find out what I can, sir. The dressing bell has just gone. We have our new tailored suit."

"We, Becket?"

"I understand that is the way menservants talk, sir."

"Don't do it. It reminds me of the nursery."

"Very good, sir."

At the dinner table, Harry covertly studied the other guests. Rose was looking beautiful in a creamy-white evening dress trimmed with spotted net frills and baby ribbon. She caught him looking at her and gave him a hard stare before turning to Freddy Pomfret on her right.

Harry gave a mental shrug and addressed Mrs. Jerry Trumpington, seated on his left.

"Bad business," he began.

"Oh, it'll be over soon," said Mrs. Trumpington indistinctly through a mouthful of quail. "Fuss about nothing."

"So you think it was an accident?"

"Of course. Parents are abroad but heading back fast. Pity for them. Still, it couldn't be anything else. Unless you can be murdered for being a dismal failure at your first season. Which is exactly what all these girls were—except the Americans. Great dowries. They'll go fast. And Hedley will have made a bit of money out of it."

"Money? How?"

"Yes, but more, more." Mrs. Trumpington broke off to address a footman serving fish.

"Ah, where was I? Ah, yes, the men are paying for a chance at the Americans and the gels' parents are paying in the hope that their daughters will make a match."

"I would not have thought our host needed the money."

"Greedy. That's what he is." Mrs. Trumpington filled her mouth with fish.

Harry turned to Miss Maisie Chatterton on his other side. "Are you bearing up," he asked her.

"Yeth," whispered Maisie. "I telephoned Mama and told her to come and get me and she wouldn't 'cos she thaid that a drama like this would bring out the knight errant in the gentlemen and get me a proposal."

"And has it?"

"No, they're all after the Americans. 'Snot fair. They're not Bwitish."

"Did you know Miss Gore-Desmond well?"

"No."

"Was she hoping for a husband?"

"Odd. She said she didn't need to look. Was already spoken for."

"By whom?"

"Don't know. You're as bad as the police. All these questions." Maisie giggled and rapped him on the arm with her fan.

Dinner was a shorter affair than usual. The men spent very little time over their port and cigars before joining the ladies in the drawing-room.

Harry found himself drawn to Rose's side. "Captain Cathcart," she said coldly, "why are you here?"

"Late guest."

"I do not believe it. I believe Hedley wants you to use your grubby skills to get rid of the police. What are you going to do? Blow up the castle?"

"I hadn't thought of that. Do you think it murder?"

"I don't know. When did you arrive?"

"This afternoon. I have a splendid new motor car, a Lanchester."

"Nasty, smelly things. It's a fad. It'll never catch on."

"Lady Rose. The horse is a thing of the past. Some of the cabs in London are already motorized."

"Of almost twenty-five thousand vehicles which passed along Piccadilly in one day of this year," said Rose, "less than four hundred were motor cars. Now what does that tell you?"

"It tells me that you have a fantastic memory for facts, and that memory of yours has led you to believe your intelligence superior. I think you are showing off. I think that desire to show off has blinded you to the obvious fact that the motor vehicle is here to stay."

Rose walked away from him, her face flaming. Margaret came to join her. "The handsome captain appears to have insulted you."

"He's insufferable," hissed Rose.

"What did he say?"

"He insists the motor car is here to stay."

"He's quite right. Was that all?"

Rose suddenly felt she had made a fool of herself. "Oh, he said other things. How are you?"

"Worried. I cannot find Colette. I had to dress myself for dinner. Do you think your maid might know where she is?"

"I'll find out," said Rose. She summoned a footman and told him to fetch Daisy.

She waited until Daisy entered the drawing-room and she and Margaret went up to her.

"Colette is missing," said Margaret. "Do you know where she is?"

"Colette didn't appear for dinner in the housekeeper's room," said Daisy. "So the housekeeper sent one of the maids to her room but she wasn't there."

"Does she have a room off yours?" Rose asked Margaret.

"No, you were favoured."

"I know where it is," said Daisy.

"Would you please go there and find out if her belongings are still there?"

Daisy bobbed a curtsy and left the room.

"Has she ever disappeared before?" Rose asked Margaret.

"Never."

They waited impatiently until Daisy reappeared. "Her clothes are gone and her suitcase," she said. "Why would she go like that?"

Margaret sighed. "I'll need to engage another. May I share Daisy with you?"

Daisy and Rose exchanged startled looks. Daisy had learned a great deal quickly but was far from being a perfect lady's maid, but Rose did not know how she could possibly refuse her new friend.

"Of course," she said. "You may go, Daisy."

Daisy had just left the room when she heard a voice behind her, calling her name. She turned round and saw the tall figure of Harry Cathcart, who had just emerged from the drawing-room.

She bobbed a curtsy. "Sir?"

"I overheard something about a missing lady's maid."

"That's Colette, Miss Bryce-Cuddlestone's maid."

"When did she disappear?"

"Today, sometime or another, sir."

"Would you please take me to her room?"

"Follow me, sir."

Daisy, who knew that the captain had been brought to Stacey Court to deter the king's visit, having been part of the plot herself, shrewdly guessed he had been summoned by the marquess to help to subdue any scandal. Servants' gossip had also informed her that it was Captain Cathcart who had found out what a cad Blandon was.

They reached the servants' quarters at the top of the castle, stopping on a landing to pick up and light candles, gaslight not extending to the servants' rooms. Daisy led the way along an uncarpeted corridor and pushed open a door.

"Why did she have a room of her own?" asked Harry. "There are so many visiting servants."

"This is one of the smallest and her mistress was one of the first arrivals."

Harry looked around. A cupboard with a curtain over it to serve as a wardrobe, a chest of drawers, a narrow bed, a table and chair, and a hooked rug beside the bed on bare floorboards.

Daisy held back the curtain over the cupboard. "See! All her clothes have gone."

Harry set his candle in its flat stick on the table. He opened the top drawer of the chest of drawers and then the lower ones.

He turned again and surveyed the room. Then he went over to the bed, stripped off the covers and threw them on the floor, and then pulled up the thin mattress. "Bring the candle over here," he ordered.

Daisy held her candle high as she joined him. Lying under the mattress was a silver locket, a cigarette case, and a piece of fine lace.

"Do you think she stole those items?"

"I think she put them there for safekeeping," said Daisy. "Lady Rose gave me a bracelet and I keep it under my mattress here in case anyone tries to steal it."

"Odd," said Harry. "Did you ever talk to her?"

"Only a little when our ladies were out for a walk. She was talking about morals and saying about the cards on the bedroom doors being there so that the gentlemen would know which room to visit during the night. But she said young ladies were strictly protected. I said that since the party was mostly young ladies, there'd be no goings-on. Something like that. And she said, 'But some of them can fall. I know . . .' And then Miss Bryce-Cuddlestone called for her shawl, so I never did find out what she was talking about."

Harry stood still for a moment. Then he replaced the mattress and the bedclothes. "You'd best keep quiet about this for the moment," he said.

"If Miss Gore-Desmond was murdered and Colette knew something and was maybe paid to go away," said Daisy, "you wouldn't cover up something like that, sir?"

"No, I couldn't. Is the superintendent resident in the castle?"

"No, sir, he's at the Telby Arms."

"I'd better see him sometime early tomorrow morning," said Harry, half to himself. "That will be all, Daisy. Let's go."

They left the room and began to walk back along the corridor and downstairs.

"Why did you decide to become a lady's maid?" asked Harry.

"Lady Rose offered me the job."

"And do you like it?"

"Yes. Ever so."

"Is anyone courting Lady Rose?"

"Not yet. But they will."

"Yes, I suppose she will not stay single for long. Society has short memories."

Although Daisy had promised not to say anything, she thought that promise only concerned the other servants and so told Rose what had happened.

"This is fascinating," said Rose when she had finished. "Do you know what time Captain Cathcart plans to leave in the morning?"

"I could find out from Becket, his manservant."

"Would you do that, Daisy?"

"I'll try. But if he's retired for the night, I can't go to the men's quarters."

"See if you can find him."

Daisy went downstairs to the kitchens where the staff were preparing dishes of sandwiches. "Has anyone seen Becket? Captain Cathcart's man?"

"His master has just rung for him," said the butler.

Daisy went back upstairs from tower to tower, studying the names on the doors until she found the right one. She retreated a little way and hid in an alcove. At last, she heard the door opening and Becket's voice saying, "Seven in the morning. Certainly, sir."

Daisy moved out of the alcove. "Mr. Becket," she whispered. "I need to talk to you."

Harry stood in the courtyard in the morning, waiting for Becket to bring the motor car round.

"Good morning, Captain Cathcart."

He started and turned round. Rose was standing there, heavily veiled, accompanied by Daisy.

"Why are you about so early, Lady Rose?" he asked.

"To accompany you to see the superintendent."

Harry glared at Daisy, who blushed and muttered, "I only told my lady."

"And why should you want to see the superintendent?"

"Because I can be of help," said Rose. Although outwardly

calm, Rose was inwardly frightened he would refuse. She was sure he had been invited to try to hush things up and she was determined to see that he did not do so.

He stood looking at her thoughtfully. Then he said, "You may be of use. But do not interrupt when I am talking to the superintendent."

Superintendent Kerridge was just sitting down to a breakfast of black pudding, kidneys, and bacon and eggs when the landlord informed him that there was a party from the castle to see him.

"Send them in," ordered Kerridge.

He stood up as Harry and Rose entered the room. "May I offer you something?" asked Kerridge.

"No, we will breakfast later," said Harry.

Kerridge waited until they had seated themselves at the table. He studied the captain. Where was the silly ass he had interviewed in Chelsea? This version of Harry Cathcart looked hard and intelligent. He was determined to go on eating. I mean, he thought bitterly, that was the upper classes for you. Drop in and interrupt a good breakfast when it suited them. Well, come the revolution, they'd be singing a different tune. Did they ever stop to think that the food that was no doubt being laid out in the breakfast room of the castle would be enough to feed the poor of this village for months? No, not them.

"You are sneering, Mr. Kerridge," commented Rose.

Kerridge flushed a guilty red. "Bad tooth, my lady. Now, what is the reason for your visit?"

Harry told him about the disappearing lady's maid and of Daisy's brief conversation with her.

"Servants disappear the whole time," said Kerridge.

Harry then told him about the items hidden under the mattress.

"The thing is," said Kerridge after he had defiantly munched a kidney, "I do not understand your interest in this. It is not your lady's maid, Lady Rose."

"I think she has been murdered because of what she knew," said Rose. "I think you should get men from the new fingerprint bureau down here to dust Colette's room. Then you can fingerprint everyone in the castle. The captain's fingerprints will be there, of course, as will those of my maid, but you can eliminate them."

"My lady, I am charmed by your interest in modern police methods," said Kerridge, pointing a sausage impaled on a fork at her, "but what will happen is this. Lord Hedley, I am sure, has phoned several people in high places. Later today, I will be told to close the case."

"But the doctor will not sign the death certificate!" exclaimed Rose.

"No doubt, given the right pressure, the police pathologist will. Deaths from cosmetic arsenic are quite common."

"But Colette . . . ?"

"A lady's maid? A *foreign* lady's maid? A *French* lady's maid?"

"I will be open with you, Superintendent," said Harry.

"About time, if I may say so, sir. You played the fool very well when I saw you before about the bombs at Stacey Magna."

"Oh, that," said Harry with a dismissive wave of his hand. "Forget that. This is important. I have been summoned here by Hedley to hush this up."

"Why you?"

"I am considered diplomatic."

"So why didn't you keep the maid's disappearance to yourself?"

"I cannot condone murder, Mr. Kerridge."

Kerridge sighed. "I will do my best in the short time I am

sure I have got left. But you can forget about fingerprinting the guests, Lady Rose. Can you imagine the outcry? I wish to keep my job."

"I would have thought a desire to right a wrong and bring a criminal to justice would be more important than your job," snapped Rose.

"Oh, really? And then what? You lot don't live in the real world. While you're up there stuffing your faces, people in this village are starving."

"You forget yourself," admonished Harry.

"He is quite right," said Rose. "The superintendent shall have our help. I shall find out what I can from the female guests, and you, Captain, can concentrate on the men. Daisy and Becket can find out what they can from the servants."

"We will do what we can," said Harry with a note of irritation in his voice, for he felt Rose was being downright unwomanly. "I would advise you to keep your radical views to yourself in future, Superintendent, particularly in the presence of ladies."

"Oh, tish," said Rose with a dismissive wave of her hand.

"They're up there a long time," said Daisy to Becket as they sat in the empty taproom.

"How do you like being a lady's maid?" asked Becket.

"It's all right. But so much to learn. I've got to wash my lady's silk stockings and I'm frightened I'll damage them."

"You wash them with soap and water and simmer them gently. For a blue shade, put a drop of liquid blue in a pan of cold spring water and run the stockings through this for a minute or two, and dry them. For a pink dye, same process but with one or two drops of pink dye. For a flesh colour, add a little rose-pink in a thin soap liquor, rub them with a clean flannel and mangle them."

" 'Ere!" cried Daisy, her Cockney accent to the fore. "I didn't think I needed to colour them. And how do you know all this?"

"I had never been a gentleman's gentleman before, so I read a great deal on the subject. I often found myself reading advice to lady's maids as well."

"What about corsets?"

"You take out the steels in front and sides, lay them on a flat surface and use a small brush and a lather of white Castile soap to scrub the corsets. Run under cold water and leave to dry. Don't iron."

"You're a mine of information. Do you think Colette was murdered?"

"If she knew something, someone might have paid her to go away," said Becket.

After Harry had driven them back to the castle, he helped Rose to alight and asked curiously, "Do you think you will like detective work?"

"Perhaps."

He smiled down at her, a smile which illuminated his normally harsh face. "Why are you so interested in helping me?"

"I would like to give you a worthy motive," said Rose. "It is simply because I am bored."

The light went out from his face and his eyes had the old shuttered look.

Daisy followed Rose up the stairs to their room. "My lady," said Daisy, "It may not be my place to say so, but you must learn to flirt."

"Why?"

"Because one day a handsome man's going to come along and someone else is going to snap him up."

Rose looked amused. "Why are you so suddenly interested in my lack of flirting?"

"It was when the captain asked you why you were helping him and he had ever such a nice smile, my lady, and you said it was because you was bored."

"What should I have said?"

"You could have said it in a jokey sort of voice and dropped your eyelashes like this and then given a little smile."

"I am not romantically interested in Captain Cathcart."

"Would do to practice on."

Rose sat down in front of the dressing-table mirror and stared moodily at her reflection while Daisy took the pins out of her hat and removed it.

"You know, Daisy, it is this pressure of marriage which annoys and depresses me. There are women in London earning their living."

"Not ladies."

"There are respectable middle-class ladies working in offices. There is nothing up the middle classes. They have sound moral values," said Rose as if commenting on some obscure tribe of Amazonian Indians.

"If you say so, my lady."

"I will now go down to breakfast and see what I can find out. I will start with my new friend, Miss Bryce-Cuddlestone."

"Don't get too friendly, my lady. She could have murdered that Gore-Desmond woman herself."

"Nonsense."

"Poisoning's a woman's game."

SEVEN
✢

It would be impossible to read poetry properly in these upper-class accents;
they have such a wretched poverty of vowel sounds: Aw waw taw gaw,
they seem to be saying. Much of this yaw haw *comes down to us from the*
drawl of the fashionable Mid-Victorian 'swells', who were suggesting to
their listeners that they were doing them a favour by talking to them at
all.

—J. B. PRIESTLEY, *THE EDWARDIANS*

In the breakfast room, Rose helped herself to kidneys and bacon
and took a seat next to Margaret.

"Have you heard any news of Colette?" she asked.

"Not a word."

"You should tell the police."

"They will not be interested."

Rose hesitated and then said, "I told them myself."

Margaret stared at her. "When?"

"This morning."

"Why?"

"A girl is missing. Under the mattress in her room was found
a silver locket, a piece of lace and a cigarette case."

"Those are items I gave to her."

"Why would she leave them behind? Someone could have

packed up her belongings to make it look as if she had left. Besides, she told my maid, Daisy, that she knew something about one of the young ladies here, implying that one was having an affair."

Margaret's face was stiff with outrage. "I find your poking around in things that do not concern you distasteful, to say the least. Now, if you will excuse me . . ."

Rose watched her go with dismay. What had she done wrong? Surely it was only natural to want to know what had become of the girl. She suddenly felt very alone again.

She saw Harry, who had just entered the room. She waited until he had helped himself to a frugal breakfast of toast and coffee and called to him, "Captain Cathcart!"

Harry joined her and said, "You are looking distressed."

Rose told him about her conversation with Margaret.

"I wouldn't read too much into it," he said. "You will find all the guests want to forget about the death of Miss Gore-Desmond. They are certainly not going to trouble their heads about one missing lady's maid. Perhaps Miss Margaret Bryce-Cuddlestone fell from grace herself with one of the men here."

"Surely not. Surely it is only married ladies who . . ." Rose blushed. Then she recovered and said, "I am sharing Daisy with her. Daisy might find out something."

"It's worth asking her if she can find out anything. It would explain Miss Bryce-Cuddlestone's attitude to her maid's disappearance."

"Morning, Lady Rose . . . Cathcart," said Harry Trenton, sitting down opposite them, a plate laden high with food. "Jolly fine weather. Nip in the air, what."

"Haven't been awake long enough to notice," drawled Harry.

Other guests began to come into the dining-room. Rose noticed the change in Harry. He seemed to have an endless fund of vacuous remarks. Perhaps that was how he found out things, she thought. People would slip their guard if they thought they had nothing to fear.

Daisy helped Margaret change into a new outfit for lunch. She was feeling more confident because Becket had told her that any fine items which needed to be cleaned by the lady's maid rather than given to laundresses were to be brought to him and he would help her.

"Have you been with Lady Rose for long?" asked Margaret.

"Not long," said Daisy. She had been primed by Rose to find out about Margaret but had not expected Margaret to want to find out about her.

"And before that?"

"I am the daughter of one of the tenant farmers on the Stacey Court estates," lied Daisy. "I am well-educated and it was Lady Hadshire's kind way of giving me a start in life."

To her relief that seemed to satisfy Margaret. "Do any of the gentlemen here please you, madam?" asked Daisy.

"Know your place, my good girl, and do not ask impertinent questions. The lace on my oyster satin dinner gown is soiled. Please have it cleaned by this evening."

"Yes, ma'am."

"Hand me my gloves. You may go to your mistress now."

Daisy held the door open for her, collected the dinner gown and took it downstairs. Rose had said she had no intention of changing for lunch and that she thought the ritual of changing at least six times a day exhausting and silly.

She went in search of Becket, who looked up his books and told her to make a lather of Castile soap, clean the lace with a fine brush after it had been unpicked from the gown, put a little alum in clean water to clear off the suds, iron it with a cool iron and then stitch it back onto the gown again.

As she worked, Daisy told him that she had been instructed to find out all about Margaret.

"If you want to find out who is sleeping with whom," said Becket, "you have to watch the corridors at night."

"What if I'm caught?"

"Just say your mistress can't sleep and wants some warm milk and you lost your way. This place is a rabbit warren. They'll believe you."

"A murderer wouldn't," said Daisy with a shiver.

During afternoon tea when the men had returned from shooting and the ladies were fluttering around them, the marquess entered.

"Good news," he said. "It has been confirmed that Miss Gore-Desmond's death was suicide. The coroner's inquest is tomorrow. There is no need for any of you to attend. We can put the whole matter behind us."

Harry followed him out of the room. "So my services are not required?"

"Glad to say they're not. But stay on. Be a guest."

"Thank you. Perhaps I will stay for a few days."

Harry rang for Becket and told him to bring the car round. Then, taking over the wheel himself, he drove to the Telby Arms.

He found Kerridge in his room.

"Been called off?" he asked.

"The marquess must have powerful connections. But it happened just as I thought it would. I've got a friend in the pathology lab. Miss Gore-Desmond had taken a massive dose of arsenic. Couldn't possibly have been a mistake with cosmetics. So a murder is being hushed up. You must be pleased."

"On the contrary. I am staying on for a few days. If I find out anything, I'll let you know."

"The coroner will bring a verdict of accidental death. I will be constrained to say I found no evidence of foul play. Then I will leave directly afterwards and return to booking and charging the lower classes who cannot pull strings."

"Makes you a bit bitter, does it?"

"You have no idea. But if you could find anything to pin this murder on any of them, I'd be very grateful. Here is my card."

"A word of warning," said Harry. "Do not spout off your radical views to all and sundry. You are lucky that Lady Rose is an intelligent woman. What if word of your views got back to your superiors?"

"I'll be careful," said Kerridge. "To tell the truth, I don't know what came over me. Maybe it was the poverty of this village. The inn's all right, but have you seen the houses? Little more than hovels."

"He's a bad landlord," said Harry with a sigh. "Maybe something can be done about it."

Daisy prepared Margaret for bed. Rose had said she could put herself to bed. She brushed down her hair and reached for the cotton-wool pads and wash to clean the make-up from Margaret's face, thinking it odd that a débutante should wear make-up at all, even though it had been skilfully applied.

"That will be all, Daisy," ordered Margaret. "You may leave. I will not be requiring your services again. Lady Trumpington has kindly offered me the services of her lady's maid, who is more experienced than you."

Daisy went out into the corridor and began to look for hiding places. She found a chest for storing linen in one of the embrasures in the corridor and managed to squeeze down behind it.

She heard the stable clock chime midnight. She heard the last of the guests going up to bed. By one o'clock her eyes were beginning to droop and she fought to keep awake.

She struggled with sleep until the clock chimed two, and was about to give up when she heard a furtive footstep at the end of the corridor.

Daisy was frightened to raise her head above the chest, but looking up, she saw a large shadow racing ahead of someone carrying a candle. Then there came a soft knock on Margaret's door.

Daisy slowly raised her head above the chest, just in time to see the Marquess of Hedley disappearing into Margaret's room. She waited until the door had closed behind her. Feeling stiff and cramped, she eased herself out from behind the chest.

She crept over to the door and listened. She could hear the murmur of voices and then Margaret's laugh, but could not make out any words.

Afraid of being caught, Daisy decided to beat a retreat.

She was bursting with news and felt she could not bear to wait until the morning. Daisy shook Rose awake, hissing, "You'll never believe it."

Rose struggled up against the pillows. "What has happened? Another death?"

Daisy perched on the bed, her eyes alight with excitement. "Lord Hedley went in to Miss Bryce-Cuddlestone's bedchamber at two in the morning!"

"Perhaps she was ill?"

"Garn!"

"Daisy! You must remember to behave like a proper lady's maid!"

Daisy was tired. "Look, my lady, a proper lady's maid don't have to spend the night listening at doors. Like being a proper detective means finding out things for yourself."

Rose's eyes blazed with anger. And then she sank back against the pillows with a sigh. Daisy had made her feel guilty. Daisy had made her feel that she was merely playing at being a detective while delegating the hard work to someone else.

And why should she expect Daisy to behave like a conventional servant when the very reason she liked the girl was because of the fact that she was not conventional at all.

"You are right, Daisy. But I am shocked. How on earth can Margaret hope to find a husband when she is . . ."

"Damaged goods?"

"Quite."

"I believe some ladies say it got broke when they were out riding."

"Broke what?"

"You know. The thing that keeps you a virgin. Sounds like hymn books."

Rose shifted awkwardly. "Never mind that. If Margaret has fallen from grace, then it stands to reason that Mary Gore-Desmond might also have been having an affair."

"There's another thing," said Daisy eagerly, "what I heard in the servants' hall."

Rose was about to correct Daisy's grammar but decided against it. The idea of escaping to London and working for a living was growing in her mind. Like herself, Daisy was now an excellent typist. They could go together. And if that happened, they would be equals. On the other hand, Daisy would need to speak properly if she were to become a businesswoman.

"Do you want to hear what I have to say, or not?" asked Daisy.

"Go on."

"Lord Hedley's pa blew the family money building this monster of a castle. Lady Hedley's the one with all the money. Her lawyers tied it up in the marriage settlements so he can't get his hands on it until she's dead. What if Lord Hedley was playing fast and loose with Miss Gore-Desmond and she threatened to tell Lady Hedley? There's a reason for murder."

"It's a reason for Lord Hedley to murder his wife. Of course, had it been Lady Hedley who had been found dead, perhaps he would be suspected right away. I think we should communicate your findings to Captain Cathcart."

"Thought you didn't like him."

"Whether I like him or not is beside the point. He has the experience we need. Good night, Daisy. You did well."

"I'm sorry I forgot my place, my lady."

"You may behave as an equal when you are with me, but not in public. I have plans for us."

"What plans?"

"I'll tell you when I have worked it all out."

Harry was handed a note by Becket the following morning. It said: "Please meet us in the library at nine. We have news for you. Rose Summer."

Harry showed it to Becket. "We? I wonder who the other person is?"

"I should think it would turn out to be her lady's maid, Daisy."

"But one does not say *we* when talking about a servant. I mean, a lady's maid is a fashionable shadow."

"I think Lady Rose and Daisy are more in the way of being friends."

"What an odd girl she is, to be sure. You'd better come along as well."

When they entered the library, it was to find both Rose and Daisy waiting for them.

"I suggested we meet here," began Rose, "because I doubt if anyone ever uses this room."

"Let's sit down and you can tell me about it," said Harry.

He sat in one chair and Rose sat in the other. Daisy stood behind Rose and Becket behind Harry.

"I think we should all sit together," said Rose. "The detective work is all Daisy's."

They all grouped around the library table.

Daisy told her story while Harry listened intently. "Well done," exclaimed Harry when Daisy had finished, and Rose felt a pang of jealousy. Not that she was romantically interested in Harry, of course. Simply that she felt she should have been the one to find out about Margaret and about the marquess's financial position. "Colette's disappearance may have had nothing to do with Miss Gore-Desmond's death. Miss Bryce-Cuddlestone may have decided her maid knew too much and dismissed her. And yet it was she who started the search for her. Anyway, I've found out some more things.

"I was talking to Maisie Chatterton. She babbles on about everything in that silly lisp of hers. She tells me that Mary Gore-Desmond said something one evening in the drawing-room to Sir Gerald Burke. Sir Gerald glared at Mary and then muttered something vicious to her, according to Maisie. Freddy Pomfret was flirting with Mary on one occasion but Maisie said that was because Mary had a large dowry. Neddie Freemantle was heard braying with laughter at everything Mary said. Maisie asked him afterwards what he had found so funny and he said Mary had mimicked the accents and behaviour of the guests brilliantly. I've forgotten the most important thing. Is Miss Gore-Desmond's lady's maid still in the castle?"

"No, sir," said Daisy.

"But surely she was kept behind for questioning by the police?"

"She left the morning after Miss Gore-Desmond was found dead. She said she would travel to the parents' home."

"What was her name?"

"Quinn, sir."

"Becket, we'd better get over to that inquest. The Gore-Desmonds will be there and with luck the lady's maid. But the fact that Colette disappeared and not Quinn is most odd. Quinn would know her mistress's secrets. What an amateur I am. I should have thought of the lady's maid right away."

"Perhaps it is because you are more used to covering things up than exposing them," said Rose.

"That was a rather nasty thing to say."

"It was not meant to be nasty. It was a statement of fact."

"Well, here's a statement of fact. You are the most unfeminine woman I have ever come across."

Becket cleared his throat. "I will bring the car round, sir. The ladies will wish to accompany us."

Becket left the room quickly before Harry could protest.

"Where is the inquest to be held?" asked Rose.

"At the coroner's court in Creinton, a market town near here."

"Very well," said Rose. "We will meet you outside in the courtyard in half an hour."

"Make it fifteen minutes," said Harry.

Mrs. Gore-Desmond's anguished cry in court that her daughter had never touched arsenic did not sway the verdict of accidental death.

Outside the courtroom the marquess was in high good humour which he tried to hide. Daisy nudged Rose's arm and whispered, "That's Quinn, the lady's maid, over there."

Rose hurried towards a tall, severe-looking woman, the very opposite of Daisy.

"I am sorry for your loss," began Rose.

Quinn curtsied and nodded. "I am surprised you did not wait to be interrogated by the police," said Rose.

"Our local police called on me to take a statement. I told them that Miss Gore-Desmond had never used arsenic for cosmetic purposes. I left to be with Mr. and Mrs. Gore-Desmond. Mrs. Gore-Desmond's lady's maid had recently left and she was advertising for another. I knew I could get the job if I moved quickly."

"Was Miss Gore-Desmond romantically interested in any of the gentlemen at the castle?"

Quinn stared at Rose from under the shadow of an enormous black hat. "I think she found them all rather silly, to tell the truth. But she was not the sort of lady to chatter to servants." The stare hardened even more, implying that Rose was one of the ones that did. "Now, if you will excuse me, my lady."

Harry went up to the marquess. "It turns out you did not need my services after all," he said.

"Good of you to come, all the same," said the marquess, clapping him on the shoulder. "Don't rush off. As I said before, stay and enjoy the house party."

"You are too kind."

"There's Lady Rose looking for you, you lucky dog." The

marquess grinned and strolled off towards his carriage.

Rose came up to Harry and told him about what Quinn had said. "At least we know she's all right," said Harry when Rose had finished. "But no wonder Kerridge gets so furious. What a shameful business. Quinn was not even called as a witness."

"So your job is over. You don't need to help to hide anything," said Rose. "All the facts have been buried as deep as poor Miss Gore-Desmond is shortly going to be."

"I have been asked to stay on as a guest and I am determined to get to the bottom of this mystery."

"I will help you," said Rose eagerly. "We are the only ones here, apart from Lord Hedley. I can start to talk about the inquest at luncheon and see what they all say during conversation."

"If there is any conversation about this death, it will be all about how it is not really necessary to wear mourning."

"If only the body could be exhumed."

"But the beauty of arsenic," said Harry, "is that it clears out of the organs very quickly."

"It stays in the nails and hair," said Rose.

It always irritated Harry when Rose proved again that she knew more about a subject than he did.

"You look very attractive in black," he said, smiling down at her.

"I beg your pardon! Oh, you feel obliged to flirt like the other men in the party. You do not have to waste time on such frivolities with me."

"Are you being deliberately infuriating, or are you just gauche?"

Rose bridled. "I think you should keep your mind on essentials. Miss Gore-Desmond may have been murdered."

"You would make a good nanny. Stop giving me orders. It is time we went back."

Luncheon was a jolly affair for all but Rose and Harry. Everyone seemed brightened up by the fact that accidental death had been confirmed. What goes on in their heads, wondered Rose. Look at Margaret, elegant and serene. How could she? Perhaps it was time to unsettle them all. She turned to Sir Gerald Burke on her right and said, "I met Miss Gore-Desmond's maid, Quinn, at the inquest. She told me her mistress had never used arsenic cosmetically to clear her skin."

"It's not very fashionable these days," he said. "She probably kept it a secret."

"I didn't think one could have secrets from one's lady's maid."

"Oh, one can, I gather, with professional, well-trained lady's maids. If you will forgive me for saying so, I notice that you are a trifle over-familiar with yours."

"I do not believe servants should be treated as pieces of machinery. They have hearts and souls and feelings, just like us."

"Nonsense. They do not have the sensitive finer feelings of their betters. They are made of coarser fibre."

"Surely that is nonsense."

Sir Gerald stared at her a moment and then turned away to speak to Deborah Peterson.

Rose decided to try her luck with Clive Fraser on her right. "I went to the inquest this morning," she began.

"How horrid for you," he said, his handsome face creased in sympathy. "No place for a lady. Still, good verdict."

"I met Quinn, Miss Gore-Desmond's lady's maid. She said her mistress had never used arsenic."

"Jolly good. Loyal servant, what."

"But I think she was telling the truth."

His eyes stared at her as if trying to solve a complex problem. Then he shook his head and said, "The weather's turned a bit sharp. Jolly castle, this. Like the ones in *Young England*. Only thing I ever read were the stories in those magazines. Knights and ladies. You must think me sentimental, but I'm a soft-hearted chap."

"Then you must have noticed the distressing state of the Telby villagers—being soft-hearted, I mean."

He goggled at her. "What about them? Tidy little pub."

"I believe the pub, like the village, is owned by Lord Hedley. He obviously favours it, but not the housing or condition of the villagers."

"Wait a bit . . . wait a bit." He banged his head. "You're one of the Shrieking Sisterhood. That's why you've these odd ideas. Pity. You being so pretty and all."

He turned away to speak to Lady Trumpington on his other side. By order of precedence, Rose should have been at the head of the table next to the marquess, but Hedley seemed to delight in the unconventionality of ignoring strict rules of protocol.

Harry covertly watched Rose repulse first the one and then the other. He felt impatient. If she would only try to flirt a bit, be a bit more feminine, she would get more out of them.

So after the male guests had set out for an afternoon's shooting, he asked Rose if she would care to go for a walk.

Soon they were walking out over the drawbridge under a steel-grey sky. Daisy and Becket were walking behind.

"I could not help noticing your behaviour at luncheon," began Harry.

"And what was wrong with it, may I ask? I was simply trying to elicit information."

"You won't get any information out of any of them if you hint at murder and go on like the grand inquisitor. If Hedley gets to hear of your suspicions, he'll send you home."

"Perhaps that would be a good idea," said Rose. "I am weary of this fake castle, its guests, and you."

"See what I mean? If you wish me to treat you like an equal—then go and boil your head, you rude . . . thing."

"How dare you speak to me like this." Rose stopped and glared at him, her fists clenched.

"You deserve it. I bet you I can get more information over the tea-table than you can."

"And how do you plan to do that?"

"By being my charming self."

"I wonder what that charming self is like. You see, I have never met it." Rose swung round. "Come along, Daisy. It is too cold. I wish to go indoors."

"What's upset you?" asked Daisy, trotting along to keep up with Rose's fast pace.

"Insufferable cad!"

"The captain. What did he say?"

"He criticized my behaviour at luncheon. He said I would never get any information if I kept hinting at murder and going on like the grand inquisitor. He even bet me he could get more information at afternoon tea than I could."

"Now, there's a challenge," said Daisy. "And I know just what you should do."

"What?"

"That pretty chiffon-and-lace tea-gown, the rose-coloured one. Then a softer hairstyle—a few tendrils escaping and lying on your neck. Your pearls."

"I don't understand this, Daisy."

"You've got to look ever so vulnerable. You twitter that you're afraid. Why? they'll ask. And you bend your neck and say in a whisper that Miss Gore-Desmond's death frightened you. You say you've always been considered psychic and are a great follower of Madame Blavatsky, raising the dead and all that. Hint that her spirit has been in touch with you."

"They will think me extremely silly."

"Oh, no, start with the ladies and you'll be amazed. Had a friend down in Whitechapel who claimed to be a medium and she charged a lot for getting in touch with the dead. She worked hard. Read all the obituaries. Had the rich coming down from the West End to consult her. 'A few more,' she says to me, 'and I'm off to America.' "

"And did she go?"

"No, the police raided her and found out all the secrets of wires under the table, gauze on wires to make it look as if a spirit was flying across the room, and they got her boy-friend as well for doing all the male voices. He was good, too. Worked in the halls as a ventriloquist."

Rose started that afternoon with the American sisters, Harriet and Deborah, who were usually shunned by the rest, who were jealous of their wealth.

Both girls had collected plates of cake and were sitting at a lace-draped table by the window. The window was of stained glass, depicting a knight slaying a dragon. Because it allowed very little light in, all the gaslights had been turned up full.

"May I join you?" asked Rose.

"By all means," said Harriet. "If I may say so, Lady Rose, you are a trifle pale."

Daisy had liberally dusted Rose's face with powder. Rose had refused white lead make-up despite Daisy's protests that Lillie Langtry used it. She did not want to die of lead poisoning.

"I know I am being silly," said Rose, bowing her head. "But I am frightened."

"Oh, the death of that poor girl," said Harriet. "Well, she did it to herself."

"May I tell you something in confidence?" asked Rose.

They both leaned towards her. "Go on."

"Have you read the teachings of Madame Blavatsky?"

"The spiritualist. We tried to, but Ma caught us with it and threw the book out of the window saying the woman was a dangerous charlatan."

Damn all Americans and their rotten common sense, thought Rose.

"You must think me such a silly-billy," she whispered, "but, you see, I have always been considered psychic, and at night I can feel Mary Gore-Desmond's presence."

Harriet exchanged glances with her sister. "Look, don't tell anyone, Lady Rose, but we've got a ouija board with us. Would you like to try? I mean, it's not as if we miss her or anything, and it will make us upset."

"You don't miss her?"

Harriet said, "She was nasty. Downright nasty. Do you know what she said to us? She said, 'Unlike me, you pair will never know whether the men just married you for your money.' I said I'd marry for love and she tittered and said, 'I can't imagine a man marrying you for anything else.'

"So I rounded on her. Didn't I, Deborah? I told her straight. No one's going to look at a skinny mean-faced person like you."

"Was she angry with you?" asked Rose.

"Not a bit. She got this smug smile on her face and said, 'I'm spoken for.' "

"Maybe someone in Derbyshire. I think that's where her home was," suggested Rose.

"That's what we thought," said Deborah eagerly. "But she said it was one of the fellows here. I say, when do we start with the ouija board?"

"Give me an hour and I'll meet you in the library," said Rose.

Upstairs, Rose rang for Daisy and told her about the ouija board. "You're lucky," said Daisy. "My friend, the psychic, had one."

"What's it like?"

"Well, the board is about eighteen by twenty inches. It's got the letters of the alphabet across the middle and numbers one to nine—oh, and a zero—in a line underneath. At the top left-hand corner there's a Yes and in the top right, a No. Down the bottom left it says Good Eve and bottom right Good Night."

"A polite board." said Rose.

"Oh, my friend told me the spirits like a bit of courtesy. Now, a little table about three or four inches high with four legs is placed on top of the board. Someone sits down next to you and you each grasp the planchette—they calls it that—with thumb and forefinger. Then the question is asked: 'Are there any communications?' The table will move around to Yes or No. Then you go on asking questions and the answers are spelled out by the legs of the table."

"But what if nothing happens?" asked Rose.

"You make it happen. It only takes a little nudge."

Daisy was sprawled in an armchair in Rose's room while Rose sat at her dressing-table. She eyed her maid in the mirror and felt a sharp rebuke trembling on the edge of her lips.

Almost as if Daisy sensed the change in atmosphere, she leapt to her feet. "I am going down to the stillroom, my lady. Mrs. Trumpington's lady's maid has made some rose-water and she promised me a phial of it for you."

"Be back in time to come with me to the library."

Daisy bobbed a curtsy. "Certainly, my lady."

The American sisters were in high excitement. "Never thought to have such fun in this stuffy hole," said Deborah. "I wrote home to my friend and said we were staying in this fake castle and she wrote back saying, weren't we good enough to be invited to a real castle? So shaming."

"You and Deborah start first," said Harriet.

Daisy gave a discreet cough. "May I suggest, ladies, that we turn down the gas and light a candle? The spirits can be very shy."

"Oh, do that now," said Deborah. "I can't wait."

"Aren't you frightened?" asked Rose.

"We've played with it before and never had anything to be frightened about," said Harriet. "Last time I asked the board for the name of the man I would marry and it spelled out Xazurt. What sort of name is that?"

Daisy placed a lighted candle on the table which held the ouija board with its little table.

"You're supposed to take the board on your lap," said Deborah, "but it's so awkward. You sit next to me, Lady Rose, and take the corner of the little table nearest you between your thumb and forefinger. As you're the psychic, you start."

"Are there any communications?" asked Rose.

To her amazement, she felt the table move. "It's resting on Yes," screeched Deborah. "Go on. Ask it something."

Rose longed to ask if Miss Gore-Desmond had been murdered but decided to ask something silly and simple. "Will Miss Deborah Peterson marry?"

The little table lurch and the leg rested again on Yes.

"My turn," said Deborah. "What is the name of the man I will marry?"

"It's moving," said Rose.

Slowly the letters were spelled out. H-A-R-R-Y.

"There's that divine captain, sis," squeaked Harriet.

"There is also Harry Trenton," Rose pointed out.

"Oh, he's so dull. Ask it for his second name." So Rose put the question but this time for some reason the little table did not budge an inch.

"It does that sometimes," said Deborah, disappointed. "Maybe we should pack it up and try another time."

"Wait," said Rose, throwing back her head and closing her eyes. "I feel a presence."

The table jerked over the alphabet and came to rest on M. Then jerkily it went on to spell out the full word—MURDER.

Deborah screamed. Harriet shouted, "Light the gas."

Daisy darted around the room with a taper until every gaslight was lit.

"That was sure a fright," said Harriet, fanning herself. "I mean, what murder? Mary's death was an accident."

"Perhaps it wasn't," said Rose, whose thumb and fingers were aching with the effort of guiding the legs of the table over the right letters. "I mean, Miss Bryce-Cuddlestone's maid knew something and she has disappeared."

"You mean Mary might have been murdered and Hedley's used his influence to get the whole thing kept quiet?" asked Deborah.

"Perhaps."

"But that's awful," exclaimed Harriet. "I say, I've read all the Sherlock Holmes books. Have you read the latest, *The Hound of the Baskervilles?*"

"No, not yet."

"I'll lend you a copy. You know something," said Harriet, "I don't think you're a psychic at all. I saw the way you moved the table. I didn't say anything because I didn't want to spoil Deborah's fun."

"Fun!" exclaimed Deborah. "I got the fright of my life."

"I think you suspect a murder and are trying to find out if we know anything. Come on, fess up."

Rose gave a reluctant smile. "I'm sorry. But I am sure there was something suspicious about Mary's death. Her lady's maid said she never used arsenic as a cosmetic to clear the skin. But if Hedley knew of my suspicions, he would send me home. I would like to find out how she really died."

"But how do you go about it?"

"You ask questions. I confess I have been very bad at it so far. I have been too direct with the gentlemen. I do not really know how to flirt."

"How too horribly sad," said Harriet. "But we do, don't we, sis? We're the best flirts in America. And if this lot here think we're going to waste our dowries on them, they're mistaken. I want a duke. It would be fun."

"I think she might have been having an affair," said Rose.

"What? That mousy little thing? You mean, one of the men did her in?"

"Perhaps. Or a jealous woman. Your lady's maids might have heard something."

The sisters' faces were immediately marked by the same looks of hauteur. "We do not converse with our servants," said Harriet. "Too vulgar. Anyway, we'll flirt with the men and see what we can find out. You haven't seen us in action because we didn't figure there was anyone worth bothering about. But just you wait until this evening."

Rose thought the sisters were in splendid form after the gentlemen joined them in the drawing-room after dinner. They flirted, they chatted, they flattered, until they were surrounded by a group of adoring men.

When she had all their attention, Deborah said, "We had such a fun time today. Lady Rose is a psychic."

Rose was aware of Harry's amused eyes on her. "She's in contact with the spirit world," Deborah went on. "So we got out the ouija board."

Rose stiffened. She did not want them to talk about murder.

"And what did the spirits tell you?" asked Freddy Pomfret.

"I'm going to marry someone called Harry," said Deborah.

"That's either Harry Cathcart or Harry Trenton," said Freddy.

"Or a Harry I haven't yet met," said Deborah.

Freddy addressed Rose, his eyes bright with malice, because he obscurely blamed her for having caused his recent disgrace. "In touch with the spirits, are you, Lady Rose?"

"It's not good to talk about it," said Rose repressively.

Harry Cathcart led her aside. "What have you been playing at?"

"I'm just trying to stir things up. Mary Gore-Desmond told the American sisters that she was spoken for."

"I wonder who she was referring to."

"Anyway, they are going to help; the Petersons, I mean."

"If Hedley knows what you're about, you'll be sent home."

"I don't think they'll tell anyone. What did you find out?"

"That Quinn was less than honest with us. She confided to Miss Maisie Chatteron's lady's maid that she was thinking of applying for a new position. When asked, she said that a mistress's behaviour reflected on the lady's maid and she had no intention of having her career damaged."

"So she knew Mary Gore-Desmond was having an affair," exclaimed Rose. "You must motor over to Derbyshire tomorrow and ask her for the identity of the lover."

"I already planned to do that."

"I shall come with you."

"I would prefer to go alone."

"Nonsense. You would be better to have me along with you to provide an air of respectability."

"You are not regarded as the epitome of respectability—or had you forgotten?"

"You cannot leave me out."

"Oh, very well. We'll set off at seven in the morning before the others are awake to ask questions. Becket has found out the Gore-Desmonds' address."

Daisy sat in a shadowy corner of the hall. Freddy Pomfret and Tristram Baker-Willis came out of the drawing-room and moved over to the fireplace to light cigarettes.

"So our Lady Rose is psychic," sneered Freddy. "Never heard such a load of rubbish."

"Wouldn't it be fun to haunt her," said Tristram.

"I say. Sheets and clanking chains and wailing?"

"No, you don't want to rouse the others. Just white face, white-powdered hair and point accusingly. No, think again. I've got it. Our bed sheets with holes cut in them for eyes."

"She'll scream and everyone will come running."

"Tell you what, old boy, I'll do the ghost bit, glare accusingly, and then we flee down the backstairs and hide until the fuss is over."

"What larks! When'll we do it?"

"About one o clock."

Rose, on entering her room that evening, found her maid in a high state of excitement. "Mr. Pomfret and Mr. Baker-Willis are coming to haunt you!"

She told Rose what she had overheard.

"Thank goodness you found out what they were planning to do," said Rose. "I'll lock my door and they can haunt all they like out in the corridor."

"It would be great to give them a fright," said Daisy. "I could haunt them."

"No," said Rose slowly. "I could do it. I wish there was some way of making me up to look like Mary Gore-Desmond."

"There's a big hamper of theatrical stuff downstairs that they use for charades. But all you really need is a sort of sandy wig. They've got a box of grease-paint as well. I could make up your face. I was in the theatre, remember. Here's what we'll do . . ."

Freddy and Tristram, staggering a little with all they had drunk, emerged from their rooms. Each was wearing a sheet over his head with eyeholes cuts in it.

They started to mount the steps to the tower where Rose's room was located.

They had nearly reached the first landing when a figure, lit dramatically by a shaft of moonlight shining through an arrow slit, confronted them.

They stopped and clutched each other. All they could see

was sandy hair over a thin chalk-white face contorted into an awful sneer. Then one white hand materialized and pointed at them.

"Murderers," wailed an unearthly voice. "You murdered me."

And then it disappeared.

It did not dawn on the frightened pair that the unearthly apparition had simply stepped back into the unlit blackness of the landing.

"Help!" called Freddy, his voice weak and thin as in a nightmare. "Help!" shouted Tristram, finding his voice.

Their terror had made them forget that they were still draped in sheets. Frederica Sutherland, the first to come running, saw the sheeted figures and fell down in a faint.

Others came crowding the bottom of the staircase. "Take off those sheets," roared Lord Hedley. "Blithering idiots."

They pulled off the sheets. "It was just a joke," said Freddy. "But we saw this ghost of Mary Gore-Desmond."

"She called us murderers," said Tristram.

"Someone's playing a joke on you. You are both drunk."

"But we saw her," wailed Tristram. He suddenly vomited all over the stairs.

"Get to bed, all of you," ordered the marquess. "I'll deal with you two in the morning."

Rose rolled around her bed with a handkerchief stuffed in her mouth to muffle her laughter. "Oh, Daisy," she finally gasped. "How wonderful it was. And when the fuss has died down, they may start to wonder whether there really might be a ghost after all."

Daisy laughed as well. She was relieved the haunting had

gone well, and also relieved that her mistress was behaving more like a young girl and less like some sort of chilly mannequin with a head stuffed with facts.

Rose fell happily asleep that night, looking forward to telling Harry about the success of their exploit.

He was furious. "Don't you know what danger you have put yourself in?" he shouted as he drove away from the castle. Rose clutched her hat and demanded, "What do you mean?"

"I mean that they will get it out of Freddy and Tristram that they planned to haunt you. Who else would decide to give them a scare but you? And why are you screeching murder? If it *was* murder, then someone may want to silence you."

"Piffle," said Rose. "You are only angry because you did not think of it yourself."

It took them three hours to reach the Gore-Desmonds' country mansion. None of them had breakfasted, and all were feeling cold and angry.

"I am famished," complained Rose as the car moved up the drive.

"Then you should have said so and we could have stopped somewhere," snapped Harry. "Let's get this over with."

The house was still and quiet, with all the blinds drawn down and the curtains closed.

"How are we going to get a chance to talk to Quinn?" hissed Rose.

"I'll think of something," said Harry.

A butler opened the door before he had a chance to ring the bell. Harry handed him his card and asked if Mr. and Mrs. Gore-Desmond could spare them a little time.

"I am afraid the master and mistress have gone into town to supervise the last of the funeral arrangements."

"And when will they be back?"

"I do not know, sir. Perhaps later today."

"We have come quite a distance. Perhaps we might have a word with Quinn?—unless she has accompanied her mistress?"

The butler turned away and they followed him into one of those side rooms in country houses which are used for receiving farm tenants and the other hoi polloi.

Daisy and Becket found their way to the servants' quarters in the hope of food.

The room was lit by a single oil lamp. It was full of over-stuffed furniture, a large battered oak desk, and paraphernalia of fishing tackle, game bags, walking-sticks and rubber boots.

Quinn entered, dressed from head to toe in black.

"You did not accompany your mistress today?" asked Rose.

"No, my lady. My mistress has seen fit to engage another lady's maid instead of employing me as she promised. I hope to shortly have employ with a respectable family who might have a better idea of how family servants should be treated."

"Please sit down," said Harry, helping her into an armchair. "We have heard that you were not pleased with Miss Gore-Desmond's behaviour."

Quinn suddenly rose to her feet, went to the door and jerked it open. The butler was standing there. "Go away and stop listening at doors," shouted Quinn. She returned and sat down.

"I was not pleased with Miss Gore-Desmond's behaviour, no. A lady's maid is judged by the behaviour and dress of her mistress."

"What precisely did you consider wrong in Miss Gore-Desmond's behaviour?"

"It is not my place to say, sir."

"But you haven't got a place now," Rose pointed out. "Surely this family is not deserving of your loyalty."

"That's as may be, my lady. But there are some things that should not be spoken of."

Rose felt like shaking her. But Harry, who was sitting close to her, took Quinn's hand and said gently, "I trust you not to repeat this, but we fear Miss Gore-Desmond's death was murder."

Quinn sat there, unmoving, her harsh face registering neither shock nor surprise.

"We have reason to believe she was romantically involved with someone."

Harry released her hand, drew out his wallet and opened it. He took out one five-pound note and then another.

Quinn still sat unmoving.

When Harry was holding twenty pounds in his hand, Quinn said, "I'll tell you what I know."

Her hand snaked out and took the twenty pounds.

At last, thought Rose, an end to this mystery. She would not admit to herself that Harry's earlier words, that she had put herself in danger, had frightened her.

"Miss Gore-Desmond was having an affair," said Quinn.

"With whom?"

"I don't know and that's the truth."

"Then how do you know she was having an affair?"

"Marks on the sheets. *You* know."

Harry did, but Rose did not, and looked bewildered.

"Then there would be a smell of cigar smoke in the room in the morning."

"Was she by any chance pregnant?" asked Harry.

"How could Quinn know . . ." began Rose, then blushed furiously. Of course a lady's maid would know whether her mistress had had her monthly menstruation. The soiled towels would need to be collected for the laundry.

"Not to my knowledge, sir."

"Had this ever happened here? Did any man visit and did you then find the same evidence?"

"No, my lord. Miss Gore-Desmond had her first season this year in London and had the opportunity to meet plenty of gentlemen. I do not know if she favoured anyone in particular, and certainly no one favoured her enough to propose."

"At the castle, did you ever challenge her about the state of the bed linen?"

"Certainly not, sir. It was not my place to do so."

"Well, that's that," said Harry as they drove off.

"Don't you think it was Quinn's duty to inform Mary's parents about her affair?"

"All Mary had to do was deny it and Quinn would have been fired. Back to square one."

EIGHT

✢

A woman feels so tremendously at a disadvantage if her hair is untidy.
She cannot even argue until it is neat again!

—MRS. C. E. HUMPHRY, *MANNERS FOR WOMEN*

Rose felt a surge of dislike for her host as the car drove through the poor village and up to the folly of a castle. The architect had not put much imagination into his plan, she thought. It was nothing more than a giant square box with towers at each corner. She was sure the moat kept it unhealthily damp.

As they cruised over the drawbridge and into the courtyard, Rose felt depressed and frightened and very young. Why not leave, go home to her parents and the comfortable surroundings of her family home?

But somehow the very awfulness of the castle inside with its fake armour in the hall and its overstuffed and over-draped furniture in the rooms reassured her.

By the time she went down to dinner, she had persuaded herself that it did not matter whether Mary had been having an affair with someone or not. She had either committed suicide or accidentally taken an overdose of arsenic.

She chatted about trivia to her dinner companions and listened politely to their tales of shooting and fishing.

In the drawing-room, the Peterson girls, Deborah and Harriet, were anxious to know where she had been that day. Rose said she had gone for a drive with Captain Harry, who wanted to show off his new car. She refused an invitation to try the ouija board again.

She retired to her room with relief and sat down at the dressing-table. Daisy began to remove the pins from her hair.

"Any more news?" asked Daisy.

"Nothing," said Rose. "You know, Daisy, I'm suddenly weary of the whole business. Let Captain Cathcart deal with it."

"That's not like you!" exclaimed Daisy.

"Yes, it's very much like me," said Rose wearily. "I have come to the conclusion that I'm a coward. Yellow as custard. I was all for supporting women's rights, but when the scandal of my photograph in the *Daily Mail* blew up, I caved in and never had anything to do with any of them again."

"Surely there was not really so much you could have done," said Daisy, "what with your parents planning your season and being so against women's rights, like everyone else in society. If you'd gone on, they might have had you locked up."

"I'll finish undressing myself, Daisy. You may go. I'm tired. I was so sure Quinn would answer all questions and the mystery would be resolved."

"Maybe things'll look more hopeful in the morning," said Daisy soothingly.

Daisy left and Rose wearily finished undressing and went to bed. There was a note pinned on her pillow.

She slid out the pin and opened it.

It read: "If you wish to know why Mary Gore-Desmond died, meet me on the roof of the castle tomorrow at 1 P.M. Do not tell anyone, even your maid. A friend."

The message was printed in block capitals.

Rose held the little note with trembling fingers. She should tell the captain. But if someone else joined her on the roof, the author of the note might just fail to appear.

She stayed awake for hours, tossing and turning, and then at last fell asleep with the note clutched in her hand.

When she awoke, she found she had slept until ten in the morning. The memory of the note flooded into her frightened brain. Perhaps it was just that wretched pair, Tristram and Freddy, planning to play another joke on her. And yet, most guests would be at lunch at one o'clock. It would be broad daylight.

She dressed in a plain divided skirt and shirt blouse and serviceable boots. She looked out of the window. It was a cold, blustery day, with great ragged clouds streaming across the sky.

"I will go. I am not a child anymore," she admonished herself out loud.

"What's that?" asked Daisy, who had quietly entered the room.

"Oh, I was thinking about letting the suffragette movement down," said Rose hurriedly. "Do my hair and then leave me, Daisy. I won't be needing you for the rest of the day."

Rose had not wanted to ask for instructions as to how to get to the roof of the castle, but assumed if she kept on walking upwards, she would come to some sort of a door.

She walked up the main staircase and kept on walking up, ignoring the corridors which branched off to the towers. The stairs became narrower and uncarpeted. She found herself in the servants' quarters, which stretched out on either side of her at the top landing.

A footman appeared from one of the rooms and stared at her in surprise. "May I help you, my lady?"

"I wanted to get up on the roof to look at the view," said Rose. She had been told not to tell anyone, but surely that meant any of the guests, or Daisy.

"You go along to the right, my lady," said the footman, "and you'll find a door at the end. If you open it, there is a stone staircase which will take you up. Would you like me to escort you?"

"No, no, that will not be necessary. I'll go on my own."

Rose made her way along the corridor to the right. She came to the door the footman had mentioned and opened it. There was the staircase leading to the roof. There was still time to go back down to luncheon and tell Harry.

On the other hand, there would be the pleasure of solving the mystery and telling him she had done it all by herself.

Squaring her shoulders and wrapping the thick shawl she had brought tightly around her, she walked up. Another door. There was a large key in it and the lock looked as if it had been recently oiled. She unlocked the door and swung it open. A blast of cold air hit her face.

Rose stepped out onto the roof and shut the door behind her.

She looked around. No one in the immediate vicinity. The roof was flat, with four banks of chimneys sending out snakes of smoke which whirled about the roof.

Perhaps someone was on the other side of the banks of chimneys. She walked around them, peering through the sudden downdraft of smoke from the whirling cowls of the chimneys. She gasped and choked. Wiping her streaming eyes, she walked to the edge of the roof and took in a gulp of fresh air.

A low crenellated wall surrounded the edge of the roof. She

was at the back of the castle, where the walls plunged down, sheer into the black waters of the moat.

Rose turned and looked around. The smoke from the many fires seemed to be performing some mad snake-like dance, first bending this way and that, then running along the top of the roof, sent down by the chimney-cowls.

He *would* have to have modern chimneys, thought Rose. If he had put in tall, fake Tudor chimneys, the smoke would be carried away from the roof and into the air.

She turned back. There was a view of the village huddled near the castle like some poverty-stricken peasant seeking warmth.

Beyond the village, near the woods, she could see the puffs of smoke from the shotguns of the men after pheasant and hear the cracks of shot. So the men would not have been present at lunch anyway. Then through the village came Harry in his car, the car looking like a toy.

On impulse, she stood at the edge and shouted and waved.

An almighty shove in her back sent her hurtling over the edge. Rose screamed and screamed as she hurtled down past the sheer walls of the castle and straight down into the moat.

Becket was seated beside his master in the open car as they drove along the winding road which approached the back of the castle. He was gazing gloomily at the castle when he saw to his amazement a tiny figure up on the roof, waving and shouting.

"Sir," said Becket, raising his voice to be heard over the noise of the engine, "there is someone on the castle roof. Oh, my God, they've fallen."

"Where, what?"

"Back of the castle, sir."

Harry drove as hard as he could, over the drawbridge, under the portcullis, through the courtyard and sped along the tradesman's route which ended at the side of the castle.

He switched off the engine, jumped out, and started to run to the back. There was a figure struggling in the moat.

"It's Lady Rose," gasped Becket.

Harry stripped off his long overcoat, his jacket, hat and motoring goggles, tore off his shoes, and dived in.

When he surfaced it was to find that Rose had gone down again under the icy waters.

He dived and groped around until his hands grasped clothing. He pulled the body to the surface and found himself staring at the bloated features of an unrecognizable dead female.

There came a faint, "Help!" as Rose surfaced again. He abandoned the horror he had found, and swam to Rose and put his arms around her.

"Relax," he ordered. "And let me tow you in."

He swam with Rose to the bank and Becket pulled her clear. "Get Lady Rose back to the castle, and then come back here with some help. There's a dead body down there."

Rose was shivering and spluttering. Then she turned away and vomited. "That'll get some of that filthy water out of you," said Becket. He tenderly wrapped her in his master's coat and assisted her to the car.

He drove quickly round to the front of the castle. The butler appeared on the doorstep.

"Get Lady Rose's maid," said Becket, "and send for the doctor."

The butler went back into the hall and shouted orders. The marquess appeared. "What's going on?"

"You must get the police immediately, my lord," said Becket.

"Oh, Daisy, help your mistress to her room. She fell in the moat from the roof."

"Why should I get the police?" demanded the marquess testily. "There is no need to get the police because one of my guests was playing on the roof and fell over."

"My lord, Captain Cathcart dived in to rescue Lady Rose and found a dead body in the moat."

"Where? What?"

"At the back of the castle."

The marquess strode out of the castle followed by his butler, two footmen, and the hall-boy.

When he reached the back of the castle, it was to find more staff there, who had seen the drama from the windows, clustered around the captain.

Harry was kneeling by a body laid out on the grass at the edge of the moat. He looked up and saw the marquess. "You had better call the police," said Harry.

"Who is she?" asked the marquess.

"I fear it is Colette, the missing lady's maid."

"Can't this be kept quiet?"

"I am afraid not. I do not know what Lady Rose was doing on the roof, but it looks as if there might have been one attempted murder and one murder of this maid."

Rose had told Daisy the whole story of how she came to be on the roof. Changed into a night-dress, she lay in bed surrounded by hot-water bottles.

"Shh, now," said Daisy. "The doctor will be here soon."

"But there is something I want you to do for me, Daisy. It's urgent. You remember how to use a telephone?"

"Yes, my lady."

"Try to get into Lord Hedley's study and phone the *Daily Mail* and tell them about me and about the body in the moat."

"Yes, I'll do that. But why?"

"I don't want this hushed up in any way. I don't want Hedley to wriggle out of this one. And phone my parents. I want you to tell them I am all right. I don't want them to read about it in the newspapers first."

Daisy left and Rose leaned back against the pillows and closed her eyes. At least there would have to be a proper investigation now. She would show them the note . . .

She opened her eyes and sat up. The note? Where had she left it? Then she remembered she had left it on her dressing-table. She got out of bed and went to the dressing-table but there was no sign of any note.

Rose got slowly back into bed, her teeth beginning to chatter with fright. The door to her bedroom opened and she let out a faint scream.

"It's only me," said Harry. "I came to see how you were."

"Frightened."

"What happened? What were you doing on the roof?"

So Rose told her story again, ending with, "And the note's gone. I left it on the dressing-table."

"I got Hedley to phone the police. The silly man thought it could be covered up. I don't think his servants and guests are going to keep quiet about a dead body in the moat."

"Maybe . . . maybe she fell in."

"She was probably pushed."

"But why Colette and not Quinn?"

"I really don't think Quinn knows the identity of Mary Gore-Desmond's lover, but somehow Colette must have found out. Perhaps she tried to blackmail someone. Where's Daisy?"

"I sent her to phone the *Daily Mail*."

"Why?"

"Because I did not want this to be hushed up. Also, do you remember how the scandal of the bombs at Stacey Magna brought so many press and sightseers to the village? The villagers here could do with some money. I think they are starving."

"They are abysmally housed but they are not starving. Country people grow their own vegetables and most keep a pig and, if I am not mistaken, a lot of food from the castle kitchens will find its way down to the village. But there is no school and a lot of illness due to the insanitary conditions they live in." He laughed. "I am sure the *Daily Mail* will point that out."

"Daisy is also phoning my parents."

"I should think the other ladies will be contacting their parents. Lord Hedley had better expect more guests."

Daisy entered the room. "I did like you said, my lady. Your ma and pa are coming as soon as possible. I told that butler to prepare a room for them."

There was a knock at the door. Daisy opened it and the marquess and the doctor walked in. It showed that the marquess had finally realized the gravity of the situation that he should allow the despised Dr. Perriman back in the castle.

"A word with you, Cathcart," he snapped. "We'll leave the doctor to get on with it."

Dr. Perriman was a small neat man with bright intelligent eyes. He listened carefully while Rose told him what had happened.

"I am glad, in a way," he said. "It means the death of Miss Gore-Desmond might be investigated again. Now, let me examine you. Did you swallow a lot of water?"

"I did, but I think I got rid of most of it by being sick. Oh,

Captain Cathcart rescued me and I never even thanked him."

"Later will do."

He examined her, sounding her chest and feeling her pulse. Then he said, "I think you have come out of it remarkably well, Lady Rose. But I shall leave a sleeping draught with you because you have been through a great ordeal."

Rose looked uneasily at the green glass bottle he placed on her bedside table. She had no intention of swallowing any and leaving herself vulnerable to a prowling murderer.

"I did not think arsenic was used much these days as a cosmetic," she said.

"Perhaps not. But there is a great deal of arsenic around. Fly-papers contain arsenic. There was a case recently where a woman had soaked fly-papers to get the resultant crystals and killed her husband. Then a lot of old houses still have arsenic paste in the wallpaper, called Paris Green. It is also used as a treatment for syphilis—I do beg your pardon. I should not mention such a thing in front of ladies."

When he had gone, Rose said, "I might sleep. Stay with me, Daisy. Oh, someone at the door."

It was Margaret Bryce-Cuddlestone, followed by Frederica Sutherland and the American sisters.

"What's been going on?" asked Margaret. "All this running to and fro and the constabulary are here again."

Rose told her story again and then said, "They believe the body in the moat is that of Colette."

Margaret swayed and the American sisters thrust her down into a chair and put smelling salts under her nose.

"I'm leaving today," said Frederica.

"Won't be possible," said Harriet Peterson. "We've all to be interviewed by the police. I phoned my aunt in London and she's coming down here. You'd best phone your parents, Miss Sutherland."

"They're in Marienbad," wailed Frederica.

"Then send them a wire. There's been something odd about this horrible place from the beginning. No proper protocol observed. All of us changed around at meals. Bad form. Auntie's from Virginia. She won't stand for any of that nonsense."

Despite her shock and distress, Rose found herself mildly amused that an aunt from the home of democracy should be such a stickler for protocol.

With her usual forthrightness, Deborah said, "There's a murderer amongst us. Which one of us do you think it is?"

Daisy stepped forward. "Ladies, you must remember Lady Rose has had a frightening experience. I think she should rest now."

Murmuring apologies, they headed for the door. But Margaret had the last word. "If you had left well alone, none of this would have ever happened."

"What a bitch!" exclaimed Daisy when the door had closed behind them.

"Daisy!"

"Well, what a thing to say. My money's on her. Just think! If you had hit the castle walls on your road down, you'd be as dead as Colette."

"I would rather not think about that. Run along and see what else you can find out."

"I'm not leaving you! You said not to."

"Now that nothing can be hushed up, I am sure no one will dare to try anything. Oh, the door again. Get rid of whoever it is."

Daisy opened the door. "It's Lady Hedley."

"Let her come in," said Rose wearily.

The little marchioness came up to the bed and peered anxiously at Rose. "How are you, my dear?"

"I think I am going to be all right."

"Such a silly thing to do! Playing about the roof of the castle."

"I was not playing. I was lured up there by some murderer."

The marchioness shook her head. "The trouble with you young gels is that you will read cheap romances."

"But it happened!"

"Now, you don't really know what you are saying. There is no reason for you to burden the police with silly stories. That awful Kerridge person is on his way."

"I will tell him exactly what happened," said Rose firmly.

"This house party was a mistake," said Lady Hedley, half to herself. "But he thought it would be amusing."

"Lady Hedley," ventured Rose, "could you not possibly prevail on your husband to do something for his villagers? Their living conditions are dreadful."

The marchioness looked at Rose as if she had just dropped in from another planet. "God puts us in our appointed stations, my dear. God put the villagers there. I heard you were intelligent. You appear very silly."

And with that parting remark, Lady Hedley left the room.

Rose's next visitors were Maisie Chatterton and Lady Sarah Trenton. Lady Sarah said she was very sensitive and had felt a *frisson* about the time that Rose was falling off the roof.

"Lord Hedley is saying that it is nothing but a theries of accidents. You were playing on the woof and fell off, Colette twipped and fell in, and Mary took too much arthenic," lisped Maisie.

"Are the police here?"

148

"Yes," said Sarah, "asking questions and questions."

"I thought they would have been to interview me," said Rose.

"That local inspector from Creinton, he wanted to," said Sarah, "but Hedley told him you weren't fit."

"I am not a child!" said Rose. "What is all this nonsense about me playing on the roof?"

"Well, you do do such odd things," said Maisie. "Some of us think you are thweet on Captain Cathcart and you fell in so that he could wescue you."

"What balderdash! Please leave me. My head is beginning to ache."

When they had gone, Rose said, "No more visitors, Daisy, unless it is the police."

Superintendent Kerridge arrived from London that evening and asked to see Harry after he had endured Lord Hedley's tales of how innocent everything was.

This time, the detective superintendent had commandeered the marquess's study.

Kerridge had received a report from Posh Cyril about Harry's skill in solving the problems of the aristocracy.

"Sit down, Mr. Fix-It," he said grimly. "Begin at the beginning and go on to the end."

Harry talked steadily for half an hour, leaving nothing out. When he had finished, Kerridge said, "So you aren't trying to help Lord Hedley hush this up?"

"I can't," said Harry. "There is a dangerous murderer loose in this castle. If he is not caught soon, there will be another murder."

The door burst open and Lord Hedley strode in. "This is disgraceful!" he spluttered. "There's a reporter and photographer from the *Daily Mail* trying to gain access. Who told them?"

"Not anyone in Scotland Yard, I can assure you."

"You can't keep anything like this hushed up," said Harry. "You'd better give them a statement."

"Damned if I will."

"They'll talk to the villagers."

"Anyone who speaks to the press will find himself without a roof over his head."

"And that would make a good story," said Harry wearily. " 'Wicked Aristocrat in Castle of Death Punishes Innocent Villagers.' "

"I am not talking to the gutter press, and that's that!"

The marquess stormed out.

"To get back to business," said Kerridge. "I have men dragging the moat."

"For the maid's suitcase?"

"Yes, I think it was probably thrown in after her. The preliminary examination seems to indicate she did not die from drowning but from a severe blow to the head. To speed things up this time, I have a squad of detectives interviewing the guests and the staff."

"I think a policeman should be put on guard outside Lady Rose's door. I don't think our murderer will try anything with all of you in the castle, but I would like to be sure."

Kerridge turned to Inspector Judd. "See to that, Judd." He turned back to Harry. "I am told Lady Rose is too ill to be questioned."

"I think you will find, on the contrary, that she is anxious to see you. There is a rumour circulating that she was so enamoured of me that she threw herself in the moat so that I would rescue her."

"Only a cloth-head would believe that!"

"Oh, you'll find plenty of those."

Kerridge got to his feet. "I'll see Lady Rose now."

In Rose's bedroom, Kerridge pulled up a chair next to the bed and sat down. "I must say, you look remarkably well, considering your ordeal," said Kerridge. Harry, who had insisted on accompanying him, sat on the other side of the bed.

Rose told her story and ended by saying, "I know you must think I am stupid not to have told anyone. I thought it might turn out to be one of the servants."

"Have you any impression of the person who pushed you?" asked the superintendent. "Height?"

"No, it all happened so quickly. I was lucky. If I hadn't been pushed so violently, I might not have dropped clear of the castle walls, and if Captain Cathcart hadn't arrived to rescue me, I would have drowned." She held up her small white hands. "Useless," she said bitterly. "Utterly useless. I can't swim. I can't do anything. I am weary of dressing and undressing. That is all I am expected to do. Spend hours at the dressing-table preparing for the next lavish meal."

"Now, my lady," said Kerridge. "You have been very brave. It must be difficult for you."

"I always feel as if I am outside of them all, surveying some elaborate play and I do not know my lines," said Rose.

"I think Lady Rose really needs more rest," said Harry anxiously. "I think she is suffering from delayed shock."

"Sounded to me like a burst of intelligence," said Kerridge. "When I think . . ."

"Yes, yes," said Harry impatiently. "Long live the revolution. But Lady Rose really needs to recover."

"You come with me," said Kerridge to Daisy.

"Won't," said Daisy. "I'm not leaving her!"

"There's a policeman on duty outside the door," said Harry. "It's all right, Daisy. The superintendent won't keep you long."

Kerridge led Daisy into the study. He began to ask questions but then just sat back and listened, enthralled, as Daisy told him everything that had happened since she had arrived at the castle with Rose—the hauntings, the ouija board, Margaret's affair with Lord Hedley, her belief that Colette knew something, the journey to see Quinn—all the little bits and pieces neither Rose nor Harry had told the superintendent.

When she had finished, he said, "What amazes me, Miss Levine, is that there is no atmosphere of fear in the castle. No one, apart from yourself, Lady Rose, and Captain Cathcart, seems in the least concerned."

"You're right," said Daisy. "Lady Sarah will faint given the opportunity, but it's all an act."

"But *why* aren't they frightened?"

"Because they really think it will turn out to be a series of accidents. Because violent things only happen to the lower orders. The murderer must be feeling uneasy."

"I hope so. Take good care of your mistress. She's a brave girl."

The Earl and Countess of Hadshire arrived the following day. Maisie Chatterton's mother came, then the Petersons' aunt, and so the arrivals continued. A harassed Lady Hedley was glad that it was only the girls who had summoned parents and relatives.

Servants were run ragged trying to find accommodation for the new guests and for their servants.

"We should never have let you come here," said Rose's mother, Lady Polly. "Most weird. I learn there has been no proper protocol with regard to the seating at the dining-table. And when that poor gel was found dead, not even a bit of half mourning."

"Did you pay Hedley to invite me?" asked Rose.

"Pay? Why should we do that?"

"I learned that he had charged the girls' parents—the ones that were failures at the last season—for the invitation, promising to find them husbands. The men were charged for a chance at getting their hands on the Americans' dowries."

"We must leave at once!"

"We can't," said Rose. "The police are not letting anyone leave until everyone has been thoroughly questioned."

"My maid tells me a story about the deaths is in the *Daily Mail* and that the village is crawling with reporters from other papers. The castle servants must be very disloyal. The *Mail* has printed the names of all the people here."

"I am sure some of the castle servants have relatives in that run-down village," Rose said, "and one of the villagers saw a way to make some much-needed money."

"Shocking! And why didn't Hedley do something about the housing of his tenants? There is republicanism afoot, not to mention Bolshevism, and bad landlords just play into their hands. Your father has had strong words with Hedley about it."

"I am glad you are here, Ma, but I am not an invalid. I cannot stay in bed the whole time. I am going to rise and go down for luncheon."

Lady Polly listened in horror as Rose gave instructions to

Daisy to find one of her divided skirts and a plain white blouse. "You must *dress!*" wailed Lady Polly. "These are trying times. And what on earth is that disgraceful garment?"

"It's a corselet."

"Where is your long corset? A woman should be properly *boned.*"

Rose decided to lie. "The doctor said my clothes should be as loose as possible."

"Oh, in that case . . . but not a blouse and skirt for luncheon. The tea-gown, Daisy. The pink one. No padding, Rose? You will look most odd. Still, I am sure they will excuse your appearance. Perhaps a little rouge, Daisy."

"No rouge," said Rose. "And Daisy, just brush my hair and tie it back with a ribbon. I am, just for once, not going to have the weight of those pads on my head."

Luncheon was a fairly silent affair. The Petersons' aunt, a Miss Fairfax, had been overheard to say loudly and forcefully that her nieces should never have been allowed to visit such a monstrous place and the men were hopeless and dilettante. She was a large, raw-boned woman with square hunting shoulders, a prominent nose and sharp grey eyes. Her voice had an American twang, which might have been pleasing to the ear had she not used her voice to condemn everything in sight. Hers was practically the only voice raised at the table, where everyone was now seated in correct order of precedence.

Rose was seated on the marquess's left and her mother on his right. At the other end of the table, her father was on the marchioness's right and Lady Sarah Trenton's father, Viscount Summertown, on her left. Harry was with the least-distinguished in the middle of the table. He had Maisie Chatterton on one side and Mrs. Jerry Trumpington on his other.

At last, over the pudding, Margaret Bryce-Cuddlestone raised her voice. "Is there no end to this?"

Everyone looked at her. Her voice was high and strained. "Questions, questions, questions," she raged. "I'm sick of policemen. Lord Hedley, can't you use your influence and get rid of them?"

"I've tried," he said heavily. "But now the press are baying for blood, there's no way of removing Kerridge. I phoned the Prime Minister several times but his secretary keeps telling me he's busy."

Rose found her voice. "Don't you think it would be better to help the police all we can? I mean, it looks as if the maid was killed and we don't know about Mary Gore-Desmond."

Inspector Judd appeared in the doorway. He whispered something to the butler, Curzon, who approached Lord Hedley and inclined his head, murmuring in a low voice.

"Tell Kerridge I'll be with him shortly," said the marquess. "This is all I needed."

"What's happened?" asked Lady Polly.

"The maid's suitcase has been dredged up from the moat. Her belongings were all in it and it had been weighted down with bricks."

Looking down the table, Rose saw that the enormity of the situation they were in had struck all the guests at once.

And Mrs. Fairfax made matters worse. "So someone here's a murderer," she said.

NINE

You may tempt the upper classes
With your villainous demitasses,
But Heaven will protect the working girl.

—EDGAR SMITH

Bertram-Brookes was the first to find his voice. "You cannot mean one of us, surely."

"Who else?" demanded Mrs. Fairfax.

"My dear lady," drawled Bertram, screwing his monocle into one eye and glaring at her through it, "it appears to have escaped your attention that we are surrounded by servants. The lower orders, Mrs. Fairfax. All prone to violence and nastiness."

"Hear, I say," mumbled Harry Trenton, rolling an anguished eye in the direction of the wooden-faced butler.

"Seems obvious to me," said Mrs. Fairfax. "Servants seem regular enough. You lot don't."

"The weather really has turned cold," said Lady Hedley, "but the autumn colours are quite beautiful."

"Quite," several voices agreed.

"It's no use changing the subject," said Mrs. Fairfax. "Someone kills Mary Gore-Desmond. Her maid knows who it is and ends up in the moat."

"It wasn't *her* maid," said Frederica Sutherland, "it was Miss Bryce-Cuddlestone's maid."

"Oh, really? How interesting." Mrs. Fairfax glared at Margaret. "Well, if you ask me, who else would want a maid hushed up but her mistress?"

There was a shocked silence. Margaret, her face white, fled the table.

Sir Gerald Burke, his eyes alight with malice, smiled at Mrs. Fairfax and said, "Amazing. Quite amazing."

"What is?" she demanded.

"Americans are always being damned as vulgar and coarse. I never believed it before. After all, your nieces, ma'am, are a delight. But now, here you are, a prime example of everything that is coarse and unrefined."

"Take that back, you whipper-snapper!"

Lady Hedley rose to her feet as a signal for the ladies to join her, seemingly ignoring the fact that the dessert had not yet been served.

To everyone's relief, Mrs. Fairfax announced loudly that she was going to lie down.

Once the ladies were gathered in the drawing-room, Mrs. Jerry Trumpington said, "Wouldn't it be too marvellous to be like that? I mean, to say exactly what one is thinking?"

"Might start a lot of wars," said Rose.

"May I remind you all," said Lady Hedley, "that you are in a civilized household? No more ugly talk of murders, please."

Mrs. Trumpington and Lady Polly went over to speak to her. The Peterson sisters approached Rose. "When do you think we can get out of this place?" asked Harriet.

"Soon, I hope," said Rose. "But, oh, I wish we could find out what actually happened. Is your aunt usually so blunt?"

"Unfortunately, yes," said Deborah. "She's supposed to be

chaperoning us at our first season next year, but we'd better tell our parents that she'll frighten off anyone who comes near us."

"Do you think she was right about Margaret Bryce-Cuddlestone?" asked Harriet.

Rose said slowly, "I cannot imagine her doing anything so awful."

"Maybe it *is* one of the servants," said Deborah. "I mean, Mary Gore-Desmond's death could have been accidental, Colette could have broken the heart of one of the servants who got mad and hit her on the head and then dumped her in the moat."

"Miss Bryce-Cuddlestone was very upset," said Rose. "I'll pay her a visit and see if she is all right."

When Rose entered Margaret's room, it was to find her seated at the window, staring moodily out.

"I am sorry you had to endure that at luncheon," said Rose. "What an awful woman!"

Margaret shrugged and then asked, "And how are you, after your ordeal?"

"Physically, I'm well, but I still jump at shadows."

"That doctor, Perriman, is good, do you think?"

"Yes, he seemed intelligent and efficient."

"And discreet? I mean, not the sort of man to go blabbing about one's physical condition?"

"Is there anything seriously wrong with you?"

"No, I just get tired. I'm worried about something."

"I'll get Dr. Perriman for you. What shall I tell him?"

"Just tell him I want him to examine me. That's all."

I wonder if she thinks she is pregnant, thought Rose. She instructed a footman to call the doctor and returned to the drawing-room. The men had joined the ladies and were sprawled about, talking or reading newspapers.

Harry approached Rose. "You're looking worried. What's happened?"

Rose told him about Margaret needing to see a doctor, and then said, "It started me wondering whether Mary Gore-Desmond's death was in fact suicide."

"Why?"

"Well, say Margaret did spend a night with Lord Hedley and became . . . er . . . pregnant, that might frighten her. She would be ruined."

"And what's that got to do with Mary?"

"Say Mary had some bad illness or had found she was due to have a child. Perhaps that might make her take her own life."

He looked at her for a long moment. Then he said, "I wonder if Kerridge was ever given a proper pathology report."

"They would not keep such a report from him!"

"Oh, yes, they would. To the high and mighty contacted by Hedley, it would seem an embarrassing case of accidental death. I must see him. Because of this latest development, he might be able to find out more."

Kerridge looked up impatiently when Harry entered the study. "I hope you have something useful to tell me."

"I'm afraid it's speculation. Did you see the full post-mortem report?"

"No, it was sent to my superiors."

"Is there any chance of you getting to see it now?"

"I can try. What were you hoping to find?"

"Perhaps, just perhaps, Mary Gore-Desmond was pregnant and took her own life. The maid, Colette, knew who was responsible and tried a bit of blackmail."

"Captain Cathcart, I know you are trying to help, but I could do with some hard facts."

"I notice that none of our rooms has been searched."

"I tried to get a search-warrant but was assured it was not necessary."

Rose waited in the hall until she saw Dr. Perriman descending the staircase. She hailed him.

"Lady Rose," he said, "I trust you have recovered from your shock."

"I hope so. How is Miss Bryce-Cuddlestone?"

"I hope I was able to reassure her."

"What is the matter with her?"

"I cannot discuss my patient with anyone."

"Oh, of course. Tell me, Dr. Perriman, would your predecessor really have signed that death warrant?"

"No, I cannot believe he would. Dr. Jenner was a very intelligent man. Although only a country doctor, he was in touch with some of the finest medical minds in the country. He did a great deal of research on his own."

"Into what?"

"There are some medical conditions not fit for a lady's ears."

"I am not squeamish!"

The doctor smiled. "But I am and there are certain subjects that I will not discuss with a young lady. Now, if you'll excuse me . . ."

Rose watched him leave and then went back up to Margaret's room. Margaret was looking much better and even had a little colour in her cheeks.

"How are you?" asked Rose. "What did the doctor say?"

"It turned out to be nothing more than a little feminine complaint. Oh, I gather that we only need to be here for two more days. The police are going to question us all over again and at length and then we are free to go."

"Shouldn't your parents be here?"

"I told them not to come as I shall be returning home very shortly. A word of advice, Lady Rose. Do not go around poking your nose into things that don't concern you. If someone really did try to kill you, then they will try again."

Rose felt a stab of fear but she said gamely, "I really don't think anyone would dare to try anything with a castle full of police officers."

"If you say so. Now, run along. You weary me."

Rose returned to her own room to find her mother waiting for her. "Have you heard?" said Lady Polly. "We shall soon be allowed to leave."

"So I understand."

"But I have some good news for you, my dear. I have been talking to Mrs. Jerry Trumpington. She says she is amenable to taking you out to India next year."

"I do not want to go to India."

"Now, don't be a silly billy, my dear. We cannot possibly launch you on another London season. India is just the place for you. All those officers! Your father will contact the Viceroy, and Mrs. Trumpington will be on hand at all times to make sure you don't make some misalliance with a fortune-hunter."

"I am not going to go, and that's that."

Lady Polly's normally pleasant round face hardened. "You will do as you are told. You are going to India and that's an end of it. And have a word with that so-called maid of yours. She was out walking in the grounds with Captain's Cathcart's manservant. As you should know, servants are not allowed followers."

Rose paced up and down in a fury of frustration when her mother had left. The thought of being shipped out to India to be put on some foreign marriage market was abhorrent to her. And yet, what could she do?

She impatiently rang the bell for Daisy.

There was no reply, so she summoned a footman and told him to fetch her maid.

Daisy arrived, looking flustered. "I'm sorry," she said, taking off her hat. "I didn't think you'd be wanting me."

"My mother tells me you were seen walking in the grounds with Becket."

"I didn't think you'd mind."

Rose slumped down into a chair. "I am supposed to mind. Servants are not allowed followers or indeed any life of their own. Just like me."

"Something bad's happened. What is it?"

"My mother informs me that I am to go to India with Lady Trumpington next year."

"With that horrible old cow!"

"Yes, Daisy. What am I to do?"

"Maybe we could do what you thought of. Become business women."

"I am underage. They would simply come and fetch me, and if I persisted in staying, they would get some tame doctor to get me committed to an insane asylum."

"You parents would never do that!"

"They might. A girl of my class working for her living would qualify as insanity in their minds. Oh, that reminds me. Margaret summoned Dr. Perriman. I asked if his predecessor would really have signed Mary Gore-Desmond's death certificate. He said that old Dr. Jenner did a lot of research but when I asked on what subject, he said it was not suitable for my ears. What could it be?"

"Sexual problems, I suppose," said Daisy. "Like gonorrhoea and syphilis."

"How do you know such things?"

"A chorus girl down the East End has to know such things. Sometime we got some of the mashers from up west, trying their luck, particularly with the young ones like me."

"Why was that? I mean, why the young ones?"

"They'd be hoping to find a virgin, like."

"I don't understand."

"Well, they say that if a man with one of them diseases sleeps with a virgin, he'll be cured. It happened to one of the girls, Ellie."

"And what happened?"

"I don't know what happened to him, the rat, but Ellie got syphilis."

"Is there no cure?"

"I think you're supposed to take mercury, but Ellie couldn't afford doctor's bills."

"How awful. You didn't ever . . . I mean, you haven't . . ."

Daisy gave a cheeky grin. "Not yet. I've got fourteen brothers and sisters, but like the song says, we was poor but we was honest."

"Don't you miss your family?"

"Not much. Da drinks something awful and is always out of work. I seem to have worked at one thing or another since I was out of the cradle. Never mind me. What about India?"

"I'll think of something," said Rose desperately.

———

Kerridge was taking a break from interviews by walking with Harry in the grounds. Somehow he felt comfortable in the company of the captain, subconsciously sensing a misfit like himself.

"What makes you think the servants are not involved?" asked Harry.

"Because I think Lord Hedley knows something he's not telling us. I think he's guilty about something. His voice is becoming hoarse and he doesn't look well. When I first met him, he looked like our king on a good day.

"You see, the way I look at it is this. You people, you society people, lead very empty lives. Everything is given over to pleasure, and you slave at it. You don't like the up-and-coming rich from the middle classes, so you invent silly things to keep them at bay. I was served a nice bit of fish last night. 'Where's the fish knife?' I asked. That butler Curzon looks down his nose at me and says, 'We do not allow fish knives here.' So I'm supposed to eat my fish with a fork in one hand and a bit of bread in the other.

"The one deadly sin is 'Thou Shalt Not Get Found Out.' They are releasing the full post-mortem report to me. It should be arriving by messenger tomorrow."

"I admit Hedley does not look well," said Harry. "But he does not look particularly guilty either."

"Who does? Once a murderer's photograph is published, everyone says, 'Oh, look at those killer eyes,' forgetting that before that, they considered him a decent chap."

"Is there any chance of you letting me know what's in that report?"

"I'll think about it. What about you and Lady Rose?"

"What about her?"

"Very attractive girl," said Kerridge with a sly look.

"I admit she is attractive," said Harry, "but she is the most unfeminine girl I have ever come across."

"I wouldn't say that. You're dragging that bad leg of yours a bit. Let's go back."

Harry's idea that Rose was unfeminine was to receive what he considered shocking confirmation. Two hours before the dinner gong, he received a note asking him to meet her in the library.

As he made his way there, he felt amused. Perhaps Rose had formed a tendre for him. He would let her down gently.

He found Rose in the library accompanied by Becket and Daisy. He put the little pang of disappointment down to indigestion.

"How can I help you?" he asked.

"I asked Daisy and Becket to attend because it is a delicate subject. I need information."

"Go ahead."

Rose had armoured herself in full fashion. She was wearing a thin pale-green silk afternoon dress, with a trimming of dark green velvet. The boned bodice was trimmed with fine lace over green velvet. It had full sleeves and fitting inner sleeves. The wide belt round her small waist was decorated with tiny velvet bows.

Little green velvet shoes peeped out from below her gown as she drew forward a chair to sit down.

"Pray be seated, Captain," she said. Daisy stood behind Rose's chair and Becket behind Harry's.

"I think we should all sit down," said Rose. "There is no need for ceremony."

Becket helped Daisy into a chair and then sat down himself.

"I was wondering about sexual diseases," said Rose.

Harry stared at her, wondering whether he had heard her properly. "Did you say sexual diseases?"

"Yes."

"Why?" asked Harry nervously.

"It is just an idea," said Rose. "You see, Daisy tells me that gentlemen have been known to have intimate relations with virgins in the hope of being cured of, say, syphilis."

"Where is this leading?"

"Mary hinted that she had someone interested in her, that she had been spoken for. Now it would never have crossed my mind before that any unmarried young lady would fall from grace. But if a man had one of these terrible diseases, he might be very persuasive, promise her anything. Then, if she found out the truth, she might want to take her own life."

"I fear your new-found knowledge of the nastier aspects of the world is making you jump to mad conclusions," said Harry.

"Not quite. Margaret Bryce-Cuddlestone spent a night with Lord Hedley. Today she sent for the doctor. She was most upset."

"But why sexual disease? She might just be frightened that she is pregnant."

"Perhaps. But don't you see? If Lord Hedley slept with Margaret, it follows he may have slept with Mary Gore-Desmond. Perhaps she threatened to tell his wife and his wife has the money."

Harry sat silently in thought. "You don't like the idea," said Daisy pertly, "because you didn't think of it."

"Mind your manners," snapped Harry.

"Daisy was only trying to help," said Becket angrily and Harry looked at his manservant in surprise.

"So what do you suggest we do?" he asked. "Confront Miss Bryce-Cuddlestone? She will deny it. She has too much to lose. And Hedley will most certainly deny it."

"Perhaps you should tell Kerridge of our suspicions. He might get the doctor to talk."

"Shhh!" said Daisy suddenly. "I think I heard something."

She ran lightly across the room and threw open the door. She could hear footsteps hurrying off in the distance at the back of the hall. Daisy ran in pursuit and found her way blocked by Curzon. "Is anything the matter?" he asked.

"Get out of my way!" shouted Daisy.

Curzon took her arm in a strong grip. "It is time you and I had a word, Miss Levine. You do not shout at a superior servant in that manner. You—"

"Daisy!" called Rose, hurrying across the hall. "Is anything the matter?"

"I'll speak to you later," hissed Curzon.

"It's all right, my lady," said Daisy. They walked back to the library. "Someone was listening," said Daisy. "I heard these footsteps running away and went after whoever it was, but that great idiot Curzon blocked my way."

Harry looked at Rose. "Is there a constable outside your room at night?"

"Yes. Well, there was last night."

Harry turned to Daisy. "Make sure he's on duty tonight."

Rose was mounting the staircase with Daisy when Curzon came hurriedly up after her.

"Lady Hedley wishes a word with you, Lady Rose. Follow me. Alone," he added with a glare at Daisy.

Feeling nervous, Rose walked after him, wondering if Lady

Hedley had been the one listening at the library door, and then dismissed the idea as ridiculous.

Curzon threw open the door and announced her and then left them together. Lady Hedley was seated before the fireplace in her sitting-room, working at a piece of tapestry.

"Sit down," she ordered. "No, not there. Opposite. Where I can see you."

Rose did as she was bid. There was a long silence while Lady Hedley's needle flashed in and out of the piece of tapestry mounted on a frame.

Then she began. "We have not really had an opportunity to talk."

"I am most grateful to you for your hospitality," said Rose.

The needle paused. "No you're not," said the countess. "How could you be? What do you think of this castle?"

"Very fine."

"Why?"

"Well, very romantic, like castles in stories of knights and ladies."

"Piffle. I assumed you had some intelligence."

"You do not expect me to say what I really think," said Rose, becoming angry.

"It would be pleasant if you would try to do so."

Rose took a deep breath. Why should she care what Lady Hedley thought?

"All right. It is silly, a folly, and set as it is against the poverty of the local village, a disgrace."

"Still banging on about that village, hey? It may please you to know that Hedley has set about repairs."

"Yes, it does please me."

"He's only doing it because the gutter press have criticized the living conditions."

There was another long silence. Rose felt herself becoming almost hypnotized by the flashing needle.

"What did you think of Mary Gore-Desmond?"

"Nothing at all. I barely knew her."

"I saw too much of her. Did you know I brought her out?"

"No, my lady. At the last season?"

"Yes, for part of it. Her mother fell ill towards the end but was still hoping her plain daughter should make a match with someone, anyone. So we took her on. Nasty little thing."

"My lady, she's dead!"

"That doesn't soften any memories I may have of her. But the real reason I asked you here was to find if you had recovered from your shock."

"I hope so, my lady, but to tell the truth, I am afraid the experience will haunt me for some time."

"I used to play up there when I was a child when we were brought here on visits. The place was fairly new then. As children, we thought it romantic."

"I was not playing. Someone asked to meet me on the roof and then pushed me over."

The marchioness laughed. "We used to invent stories like that. It does take me back."

The dressing gong sounded.

"Run along," said Lady Hedley. "And behave yourself."

Rose repeated the conversation to Daisy. "She sounds mad," said Daisy.

"No, I think she is eccentric. It must be so terrible to have a philandering husband."

"That's mostly what this lot do to pass the time," said Daisy cynically. "But we should tell the captain about Mary Gore-

Desmond having stayed with them in London."

But Rose was not to be allowed any chance of speaking to Harry after dinner. Her mother drew her aside in the drawing-room and said, "It has come to our ears that you have been seen spending a certain amount of time with Captain Cathcart. Now although your pa is grateful to him for his help and although his family background is impeccable, he does not have any money other than the money he earns. So he is, in effect, a tradesman."

"I have no interest in Captain Cathcart."

"I will determine it stays that way."

When the men joined them in the drawing-room, Lady Polly stayed firmly by her daughter's side.

She need not have bothered. There was no sign of the captain.

He was in the library with Becket and Daisy, having had a note from Daisy passed to him by Becket.

She told him all about Rose's interview with Lady Hedley.

"It's beginning to look as if Hedley himself might be responsible for these murders, and that is going to be very hard to prove," said Harry. "But Lady Rose is surely safe. There will be a constable on duty outside her door tonight."

Curzon had supervised the sandwiches and drinks to be taken up to the drawing-room. Now all that was left was to see that the various bedtime requests were taken up to the rooms.

Mrs. Jerry Trumpington required a bedtime drink of hot milk and brandy; Miss Maisie Chatterton, cocoa; and so on. He ran his eyes down the list in his hand. At the bottom was tea, Indian, with milk and sugar for Constable Bickerstaff.

"Who is Constable Bickerstaff?" he shouted.

"That must be the officer outside Lady Rose's bedroom," said the cook.

"I think it's a bit much when common officers start using this place as a restaurant," grumbled Curzon.

He said to the second footman, John. "Get one of the house-maids to make a pot of tea and you carry it up. And take Mrs. Trumpington's drink and deliver Miss Chatterton's cocoa as well."

John collected the three drinks on a large tray and headed for the stairs. There was a back staircase in the castle for the servants, but most used the main staircase unless they were carrying down the slops. He delivered Maisie Chatterton's cocoa first and then hurried along to the other tower, where Lady Rose and Maisie Chatterton had their rooms.

He thought sulkily, and not for the first time, that the gas should have remained lit. It was difficult balancing the tray and a candle. He put the tray down on a small table in the passage outside Mrs. Trumpington's room, put the glass of milk and brandy on a smaller tray and knocked at the door. He handed the tray to the lady's maid and then turned and picked up the tray with the remaining drink from the table. He was heading up the tower stairs when he heard a voice call, "John!"

The voice was muffled and he could not tell if it came from a man or a woman. He set the tray down on the stairs and held his candle high. It was probably Mrs. Trumpington complaining again. Probably a skin had formed on her milk and brandy. She had complained before.

He ran down and knocked on her door. "Anything up?" he asked the lady's maid.

"No," she said, "and don't knock again. Madam is just about to go to sleep.

John sighed and went back up the stairs and picked up the

tray. He approached the constable who was sitting on a chair outside Rose's room.

"Are you Bickerstaff?" he asked haughtily.

"That's me."

"Here's your tea."

"That's very kind of you."

John grunted by way of reply and marched off down the stairs. He was already planning to try to find a position in a "regular" household, one where they didn't have murders or expect footmen to serve policemen.

Bickerstaff sipped the tea. It had a funny taste, but it was probably one of those foreign teas. Give him a good cup of Indian any day. But it was hot and strong and he drank it gratefully.

The tray with the tea was on the floor beside him. He bent down to pour himself another cup when he began to feel dizzy. His legs and arms were beginning to feel like lead. He slumped down onto the floor and with his last remaining strength kicked at the door of Rose's bedroom and shouted faintly, "Help!"

Rose awoke with a start and rang the bell on her bedside table. Daisy came running in, crying, "Did you hear something? I heard something."

"Ask the constable if everything is all right," said Rose.

Daisy opened the door and screamed, "He's dead! Oh, my God, he's dead!"

TEN

If this young man expresses himself in terms too deep for me,
Why, what a very singularly deep young man this deep young man
    must be!

—W. S. GILBERT

Doors flew opened, voices shouted, guests and servants came running. Kerridge, now staying at the castle, appeared wrapped in a large Paisley dressing-gown to take charge.

Once more a servant was sent to Creinton to bring Dr. Perriman. Kerridge bent over Bickerstaff and felt his pulse. Then, producing a large handkerchief, he covered his hand and gingerly lifted the lid of the teapot and sniffed.

"He's drugged," he said. "He's not dead. I want the servant who brought this tea up to come to the study and I want to interview the kitchen staff. Some of you get Bickerstaff to a bed." He turned to Rose. "What alerted you?"

"I heard a banging at my door," said Rose. "I think the poor man must have realized at the last minute that he had been drugged and hit the door."

Curzon pushed forward. "It was John, the footman, who took the tea up."

"Whose idea was it to serve the constable with tea?"

"It was on the list," wailed Curzon.

"What list?"

"There's a list in the kitchen for all the late-night drinks that people may require in their rooms."

"And who makes up this list?"

"It's pinned up during the day in the main kitchen and various valets and lady's maids write down what is required."

"Bring the list to my study. Ah, there you are, Judd. Get another officer to stand guard outside Lady Rose's door and make sure he does not drink or eat anything while on duty."

"It was probably another of Mr. Pomfret's pranks," said Lady Sarah Trenton. She had flirted with both Freddy and Tristram to no avail and was feeling rejected and sour.

"I'd better see them. Back to your rooms, everyone. I'll talk to the footman first."

Lady Polly fussed over her daughter as she helped her back into bed. "I will be so glad when we get you away from this dreadful place. I shall heave a sigh of relief when we can get you off to India with Mrs. Trumpington."

"I'm not going."

"Yes, you are, and you are not taking that so-called maid, Daisy, with you. You will have a proper lady's maid."

Rose burst into tears. Lady Polly patted her shoulder and then snapped at Daisy, "Don't just stand there. Do something."

"I think you should leave her to me," said Daisy firmly. "My lady, now is not the time to upset her by telling her she's going to India."

Lady Polly shifted from foot to foot. She had never known Rose to cry before. It was all too embarrassing.

"Very well," she said curtly.

Rose's father poked his head around the door. "Dreadful business," he said. "Place is full of murderers. I'll send for two of the gamekeepers. They'll do a better job of guarding Rose. Keep her in her room and get her meals sent up."

Rose sobbed into her pillow.

"Well . . . harrumph . . . don't cry," said the earl. "Everything will look different in the morning."

He and his wife left. Daisy hugged Rose, rocking her back and forth. "There, now, Daisy's here, and as long as Daisy's here you won't be going to India."

"They'll make me," wailed Rose.

"Not if we run away."

She handed Rose a handkerchief. Rose scrubbed her eyes and sat up. "Run away?"

"Why not? We could go back home after this is all over and really make sure our typing is perfect. Then we wait till your parents are off visiting someone and off we go."

"But they'll put Captain Cathcart on the job and he'll find us!"

"I think not, if we talk to him first. Think of it! You and me independent and free as the air, living in London."

Rose smiled. "I am feeling better already. But I wonder who was out to get me this evening."

Kerridge had taken a statement from John when a constable entered the study and said that Miss Frederica Sutherland was anxious to speak to him on a matter of importance.

"Show her in," said Kerridge wearily.

Frederica entered the room swathed in a pink satin robe. "I thought you ought to know," she began.

"Know what? Pray take a seat, Miss Sutherland."

"I saw him."

"Who?"

"Sir Gerald Burke."

"When, and what was he doing?"

"It was like this. I wanted a cup of cocoa, but it was late and the servants can get very uppity if you haven't ordered in advance."

"Go on."

"I thought I would go down to the kitchens and make myself some. I opened my bedroom door a crack to make sure there was no one about. John the footman passed me carrying a tray. I waited to make sure he had really gone but I heard footsteps. I saw Sir Gerald go up the stairs after John, and then I heard a voice call, 'John.' I thought that there were really too many people about, so I went back to bed."

"The voice that called out—man or woman?"

"I couldn't say. Could have been either. It sounded muffled somehow."

"Thank you, Miss Sutherland. We may have to speak to you again in the morning."

After she had left, Kerridge drew forward a plan of the guests' rooms. "That's odd," he said. "Burke had no reason to be in that tower. He's in the other one, the east tower."

"Maybe he was visiting one of the ladies," said Judd. "Although he looked a bit of a daisy to me."

"We'd better see him and find out what he was doing. Where's Curzon and that list?"

At that moment the door opened and the butler walked in. "I cannot find it," he said. "The list has gone."

Kerridge sighed. "Go and take another look. Send Sir Gerald Burke."

"He may be asleep."

"Then wake him!" snapped Kerridge.

After ten minutes, Gerald appeared. He held out his wrists. "Put the handcuffs on," he said. "It's a fair cop. Isn't that what they say?"

"Only in penny dreadfuls," said Kerridge. "Do sit down and tell us what you were doing in the west tower. You followed the footman, John, up the stairs. And yet your room is in the east tower."

Gerald wrapped himself more closely in an elaborately embroidered dressing-gown. He extracted a long cigarette-lighter, a gold cigarette-case and a box of matches from his pocket and proceeded to light a cigarette with maddening slowness.

"Sir Gerald. I am waiting!"

"I lost the way," said Gerald. "Simple. I was half-way up when I saw the Trumpington female's card. So easy to get lost in this pseudo-medieval horror."

Kerridge consulted his notes. Harry had told him about Lady Hedley's conversation with Rose and how Mary Gore-Desmond had been a guest of the Hedleys during the season.

He stared at Gerald, who smiled back through a wreath of cigarette smoke. Kerridge decided to take one of his leaps in the dark. "You were very friendly with Miss Gore-Desmond when she was staying with the Hedleys, were you not? In fact, her parents thought you might make a match of it."

"Ridiculous. I admit I did squire her about a bit. It was Hedley's idea. He said he'd promised her parents to try to get her engaged but he said that maybe she would look more attractive to the fellows if I could be seen paying her a bit of attention. But she began to take me seriously and I knew I'd better get out or that desperate little thing would be suing me for breach of promise or something. Too, too fatiguing. Not as if she had much of a dowry, either."

"And when you found that out, that was when she became boring?"

"Don't inflict your middle-class morals on me, my dear, dear chap. One has to look after oneself in this wicked world. My tailor's bills alone would keep someone like you in luxury."

"Were you intimate with her?"

"I do not go around seducing virgins."

"So you say the reason you were in the west tower was because you lost your way? I find that hard to believe."

"Think, dear Super, just think what this wretched place is like at night. Hedley's father went to great expense to get gas piped to the castle and now everyone who is anyone has electricity. The gaslight all over the house and in the corridors is turned off at night and we are all expected to collect our bed candles from the table in the hall.

"I turned left at the first landing instead of right, that is all. A simple mistake. I must inform you, I am known to the crowned heads of Europe and am not in the way of having my word doubted by a common policeman."

Kerridge comforted himself with a sudden vision of himself, three stone lighter, and twenty years younger, manning the barricades while the limp body of Sir Gerald hung from a lamppost.

"Sir Gerald, I would advise you to co-operate with the police. We are now looking on the death of Miss Gore-Desmond as murder."

Gerald got languidly to his feet. "Oh, do let me know how you get on. Will that be all?"

"For the moment."

Gerald swanned out. "Insufferable little tick," raged Kerridge. "I'll bet he did it."

"Doesn't look to me as if he could do anything with any woman," said Judd.

"Oh, that kind would lay the cat if there were money in it. Get the cook up here and then the rest of the kitchen staff. It's going to be a long night."

Fortunately for Rose, her mother had instructed the doctor to see her after he had examined the policeman. The sympathetic doctor reported back to Lady Polly that it would be unhealthy to keep her daughter confined to her room and might bring about a crise de nerfs.

She went down for a late breakfast. There were only a few guests present. Rose knew that her mother, like some of the others, preferred to take breakfast in her room.

She helped herself to kidneys, bacon and toast and found a seat next to Harry. He had barricaded himself behind a copy of the *Times* but lowered it and said, "I see last night's ordeal hasn't taken away your appetite."

"Do you think someone was really trying to get to me?" asked Rose.

"I'm afraid so."

"Perhaps it was just another trick by that precious pair, Freddy and Tristram." As if on cue, the door opened and Curzon announced portentously, "Mr Pomfret and Mr. Baker-Willis. Mr. Kerridge wishes to see you."

Grumbling and throwing nasty looks at Rose, the pair left the room.

"I wish that might turn out to be the case," said Harry. "But no. They wouldn't risk anything at all with a murder investigation underway. Kerridge is getting the full pathology report today. I hope he'll let me know if there was anything interesting in it."

"Have you seen Kerridge this morning?"

"No, but I saw him last night. He's probably catching up on some sleep. He wants it to be Gerald Burke."

"Why?"

"It seems Gerald was seen on the stairs of your tower instead of his own and around the right time. Someone called to John. The footman put down the tray with the tea and went back to see who was calling. That must have been the time when the tea was drugged. Mrs. Trumpington takes laudanum to help her sleep, so does Margaret Bryce-Cuddlestone. There's a bottle kept in the still-room downstairs. Poor Kerridge. There have been so many phone calls from this castle complaining to people in high places, and that includes Kensington Palace, that he is under tremendous pressure."

Curzon entered again and approached Rose. "Lady Hadshire wishes your presence, my lady."

"Can't it wait until I have finished my breakfast?" demanded Rose.

"Her ladyship said it was extremely urgent."

Rose sighed and whispered to Harry, "Meet me in the library after luncheon."

Harry nodded. Rose went up to her mother's room to find her father there as well.

"Sit down, Rose," ordered her father. "This is a bad business."

"I do not think anyone will try anything again, Pa, and we will soon be out of here."

"That is not why we summoned you. We learned that you have been seen talking to Captain Cathcart at breakfast."

"Yes. So?"

"Rose, he is not a suitable man for you to consort with."

Rose felt herself becoming very angry indeed. "Is that all you can think of? It looks as if there might have been another attempt on my life last night and all you can think of is suitable or unsuitable men."

"It is for your own good. Captain Cathcart has been useful to me, yes, but as a worker, a tradesman if you like. You are not to speak to him again."

Rose stared at them and then an idea formed in her head. A splendid idea. Blackmail.

"It would be such a pity if His Majesty were ever to learn how you engaged the services of Captain Cathcart to stop his visit. How the Kensington Palace set would throw up their hands in horror. Just think of it! My social disgrace would be as nothing compared to yours.

"My acquaintanceship with the captain is innocent. I am not in the slightest romantically interested in him. But he is the only one I can talk to about the murders. If I am reduced to confining my conversation to prattling gossip with the other men, goodness knows what I might let slip."

"You wouldn't dare!" gasped Lady Polly.

Rose got to her feet. "Well, let's see how it goes, shall we? Now I must go and finish my breakfast."

Daisy was sitting in her room. Her sewing basket was on a table beside her and a basket of silk stockings to be darned was at her feet. But she had found a bound copy of six months' issues of *Young England* in the library and was reading a serial about Roundheads and Cavaliers and felt she simply could not stop until she got to the end.

There was a knock at her door. She hid the volume under a

cushion and went to answer the door. Becket stood there. "You shouldn't be calling on me in my room, Mr. Becket. They'll all be down on us like a ton of bricks."

"Nobody saw me. The captain says he won't be needing me this morning and told me to get some fresh air."

"Amazing. It's raining stair rods."

"I don't think he noticed."

"Well, come in. But if my lady comes back you'll need to disappear sharpish."

"I've heard rumours that Sir Gerald Burke is the villain."

"That pansy!"

"You never know. He might just *look* like a pansy. He's got a nasty manner with the servants. Curzon says he's always complaining about one thing or the other."

"Curzon says! How did you get so friendly with old frosty-face?"

"He was complaining about you. He was going to complain to Lady Polly. I had to stop him somehow."

"How did you do that?"

"I said you were Lady Polly's illegitimate daughter."

"What!"

"A lot of that thing goes on. You see, most of these aristocrats have arranged marriages, so they're allowed a bit of license after the children are born. If one or the other has an illegitimate child, it's hushed up. The only shame is in being found out. Old snobby Curzon was quite melted. 'I see that must account for her free and easy manner,' says the old goat. 'Breeding will out.' "

"I don't know that I like being called a bastard," said Daisy doubtfully.

"An aristocratic one. Look at all the dukes and earls who got their titles on the wrong side of the blanket. Also, he'll never breathe a word. He worships his betters, as he keeps calling them."

Daisy began to laugh. "You are a one. I forgive you. My lady's ever so upset. Her parents are threatening to send her to India. Now what about your master marrying my mistress?"

"Won't do. He thinks she's the most unfeminine woman he's ever come across."

"If we could get them together some way . . ."

"It'll be difficult. When all this is over, she might be packed off to India and never see him again. And yet, I feel they are suited."

"She won't go to India. We have a plan. We're going to find some way to get to London and become businesswomen. We can both type."

"But that would reduce your lady to the ranks of the middle class."

"What's wrong with that? My lady says the middle classes have morals."

"My master might consider her unsuitable for marriage."

"What! A man who goes about blowing up things! He might think she's too good for him."

"I'd better go before I'm caught here," said Becket. "I'll let you get on with your sewing."

"I hate sewing," said Daisy. "I'd rather type any day."

After luncheon, Rose hurried to the library, followed by Daisy. She waited impatiently for Harry. The minutes ticked past. Daisy searched the shelves for another bound volume of *Young England*.

At last Harry entered, followed by Becket. "Any news?" asked Rose eagerly.

"Yes, very much so. Mary Gore-Desmond was not pregnant but she had secondary syphilis."

"Then all Dr. Perriman needs to do is to produce old Dr. Jenner's records," said Rose, "and the police can find out if Hedley has syphilis."

"Dr. Perriman says that Lord Hedley is not being treated by him for anything and Dr. Jenner's old records are confidential. Sir Gerald Burke's doctor in Wimpole Street was telephoned and said the same thing. His patients' records are confidential."

"Can't he appeal to the Home Secretary to get a warrant to seize the records?" asked Rose.

"I think he's trying. He says if he were requesting the medical records of Mr. Bloggs of The Larches, Jubiliee Road, Peckham, he's get them like a shot. I'm beginning to understand why he's so bolshie."

"Where are Dr. Jenner's records?"

"In Perriman's surgery at Creinton."

"Then we'll just need to get them," said Rose.

"And how do we do that?" asked Harry.

"Why, you break into his surgery and have a look."

"My dear lady, I am not a criminal."

"We could go over to Creinton. You could take me because I am not feeling well, and while the doctor is examining me, you can have a look around."

"I should think your parents will have something to say if you go driving off with me," said Harry.

"I won't ask them. Daisy can run and get my coat and hat. Becket can bring the car round. You can support me out to it and say you are rushing me to the doctor."

"It'll look odd." Harry looked at her uneasily. "Such as us always getting the doctor to come to us—we don't go to him."

"Oh, let's try!" said Rose, betraying her youth by jumping

eagerly to her feet. "Do put that book down, Daisy, and fetch my fur coat and the felt hat with the veil."

As a few of the men had gone off fishing and the rest of the guests were sunk in after-luncheon torpor, they were able to leave without any confrontation.

Creinton was a small market town and the arrival of a motor car caused a great deal of interest. Harry drew up before the doctor's surgery, which was in the main square, and switched off the engine. "If I plan to burgle the good doctor," he said, looking at the crowd which had gathered around the motor car, "I had better ride over. This thing attracts too much attention."

They entered the waiting-room. There were three people waiting, sunk in that dismal torpor engendered by doctors' waiting-rooms. This one was particularly dismal with its horsehair-stuffed black leather furniture, black marble clock and brown-painted walls.

A nurse built like a battleship came out. "Mr. Jenkins," she said, and then her eyes fell on the new arrivals, just as a small tired-looking man rose to his feet. Her heavy face creased into a smile as she surveyed the glory of Rose's sable fur coat.

"This is Lady Rose Summer," said Harry. "She has been feeling faint and anxious while we were out for a drive and I really think Dr. Perriman should have a look at her."

"Of course. Right away. Do sit down, Mr. Jenkins. Come along, my lady."

Rose wanted to say she would wait, but Harry had a hand under her arm and was urging her forward.

In the surgery, while Rose explained about feeling faint, Harry's eyes ranged over the room. Along one wall were wooden shelves containing cardboard files. As Dr. Perriman had only recently taken over Dr. Jenner's practice, they would be all the files of Dr. Jenner's patients.

He wandered over to them and then realized Dr. Perriman was addressing him. "Would you mind leaving us, sir? I need to examine the lady."

"Of course," said Harry.

He went into the waiting-room and then outside into the square where Becket was guarding the car. "I'm just going to see if there's a way into the back," he whispered to Becket. "Do you think you can hold the crowd's attention?"

"Get Daisy, sir," said Becket. "I've got my concertina in the car."

Harry summoned Daisy while Becket located his concertina and took it out of the box.

"What's going on?" asked Daisy.

"I think Becket needs your help to keep the crowd's attention away from me while I see if there's a way into the back."

Harry found there was a narrow alley running down the side of the surgery. He paused and listened as Daisy's voice, accompanied by Becket's concertina, rose in song.

> "*Come where the booze is cheaper,*
> *Come where the pots hold more,*
> *Come where the boss is the deuce of a joss,*
> *Come to the pub next door.*"

Harry grinned, remembering his tutor telling him that a Guards band had played just that song one Sunday afternoon on the terrace at Windsor castle, and Queen Victoria asked her lady-in-waiting to find out the words to the pretty air. It was with great reluctance that the bandmaster told her.

There was a tradesmen's entrance at the side. Harry studied

the door. It had four panes of glass on the upper half of the door. He could smash one and reach in and slide back the bolt, if there was one. He cautiously turned the handle. The door was unlocked. He stepped inside and examined the other side of the door. No bolts, only a large key in the lock. He extracted the key and went out and closed the door. Now for a locksmith.

A large crowd had gathered around Becket and Daisy. Daisy had moved onto a sentimental ballad, "The Blind Organist."

> *"The preacher in the village church one Sunday morning said:*
> *'Our organist is ill today, will someone play instead?'*
> *An anxious look crept o'er the face of every person there.*
> *As eagerly they watched to see who'd fill the vacant chair.*
> *A man then staggered down the aisle whose clothes were old*
> *   and torn,*
> *How strange a drunkard seemed to me in Church on Sunday*
> *   morn;*
> *But as he touched the organ keys, without a single word,*
> *The melody that followed was the sweetest ever heard."*

By asking one of the few residents who was not listening to Daisy, Harry located the locksmith and handed over the key, saying he needed an extra one to the stables.

The locksmith chatted as he ground the key, saying he had taken over the business from his father, who had died only two months ago. "Funny, I always refused to go into the business," said the locksmith, "although he trained me. But he left the shop to me, so here I am."

"What was your trade before?"

"Sort of traveling carpenter. Bit of work here. Bit of work there. There you are, sir. That should do very nicely."

Harry paid him and took the keys. As he hurried across the

square, he saw to his horror that Rose and Daisy were now standing up in the car with their arms around each other, singing at the tops of their voices.

> *"Any old iron, any old iron, any-any-any old iron:*
> *You look sweet, you do look a treat,*
> *You look dapper from your napper to your feet . . ."*

Harry hurried up the alley, opened the door and put the original key in the lock and sprinted back to the car just as Rose and Daisy were bowing before a burst of tumultuous applause.

Coins were raining into the car. Harry groaned and thrust his way through the crowd. "Show's over," he shouted. Daisy clambered into the back next to Becket, and Rose sat down in the front.

Harry switched on the engine. "Throw the money back," he ordered.

"We earned it," complained Daisy, but she and Rose and Becket scooped up handfuls of coins and threw them back into the crowd as they drove off.

"What on earth were you doing making a spectacle of yourself like that?" shouted Harry to Rose above the noise of the engine.

"It was fun," said Rose. "Tremendous fun."

"Dr. Perriman no doubt was called by his nurse to have a look at you performing and he will wonder if your adventures have turned your brain."

"Did you find a way in?"

"Tell you in a minute." Harry waited until they were clear of the town and then stopped and turned to her. "I got a copy of the key to the tradesmen's entrance. I'll go along tonight."

"I'll go with you," said Rose, her eyes shining with excitement.

"No, you most certainly will not."

"I'd be safer with you than in my room at the castle, policeman or no policeman."

"We could be the look-out," said Daisy.

"I don't know what you were about, singing music-hall songs, Lady Rose," said Harry.

"King Edward sings music-hall songs," protested Rose. "His favourite is:

> *"Hey, hi. Stop, waiter! Waiter! Fizz! Pop!*
> *I'm Racketty Jack, no money I lack,*
> *And I'm the boy for a spree!"*

"But just think if the doctor informs your parents of your behaviour!"

"Then it is up to us to find something dramatic in the records," said Rose, "so that then no one will be able to think of anything else."

Dinner was a long and tedious affair, enlivened only by the effect Sir Gerald was having on the grim American, Miss Fairfax. They were seated together and he seemed to consider all her blunt utterances the highest form of wit. The more he laughed, the more Miss Fairfax glowed.

To his amusement, Harry, on the other side of Miss Fairfax, heard Gerald saying at one point, "You really must let me take you around when we are both in London. I see you in midnight taffeta with a high-boned collar, very grande dame."

"I've never bothered about fripperies," said Miss Fairfax.

"But you must, dear lady," said Gerald. "And your hair would be magnificent if it were red."

"Wicked boy," she said with a great bray of laughter.

So enamoured was Miss Fairfax of Gerald's company that she only turned once to Harry during the long meal and that was to ask him what the hunting was like in the countryside around. When Harry replied that he did not hunt, she said, "I should have known," and turned back to Gerald.

Harry had told Rose he would leave the castle at two in the morning. He now wondered whether he should trick her and leave earlier. He had a sudden picture of her standing up in his motor car with her arm around Daisy, singing her heart out. She had looked really young and carefree for the first time since he had known her.

Lady Hedley was complaining that police had been crawling over the roof of the castle all day. "All Lady Rose's fault," she said loudly. "The young women of today are prone to fantasies and hysterics."

Rose felt like shouting a denial down the table but kept quiet. She had told Daisy to use her wiles on Becket and make sure Harry did not change his mind about taking her with him.

Daisy had rummaged in the hamper of costumes for charades and had managed to get two boys' outfits. Giggling nervously, they put them on and crammed their hair up under a couple of tweed hats. Long overcoats completed their disguise. Before they changed into their costumes, Rose told the constable on duty that she would sleep in her mother's room that night and suggested he take up his guarding duties outside Lady Hadshire's door.

Becket had told Rose firmly that if his master planned to leave them behind there was nothing he could do about it. So it was with relief that they saw the car parked on the other side of the moat. They hurried across the drawbridge, Rose clutching Daisy's arm and looking nervously to right and left.

When they climbed in, Harry let in the clutch and cruised down the slope away from the castle, not switching on the engine until they were well clear. Once out on the road towards Creinton, he stopped the car and got out and lit the headlights, climbed back in and set off again.

Rose found driving in the dark very exciting, fascinated by the square of light the two headlamps created before them.

When Harry reached the outskirts of Creinton, he parked the car under some trees, got out and extinguished the headlamps and said, "Now, Lady Rose, you and Daisy are to stay here with Becket to protect you. I will be as quick as I can."

"But I wanted to be a burglar," protested Rose.

"Stay here and don't dare move," hissed Harry.

"Spoilsport," muttered Rose. "Honestly, Becket, there was really no reason for us to come. This is not an adventure."

"It's better this way, Lady Rose. If the captain gets caught, it won't be nearly so bad as if you were found with him. Imagine the headlines in the newspapers. There are still two reporters staying at the pub in Telby."

Harry walked swiftly along, glad it was one of the days when his leg was not paining him. When he reached the square, he felt very exposed and kept close to the buildings, relieved there was no moon.

When he turned the key in the side door, the lock gave a loud click, which, to his ears, seemed to echo around the silent town like a pistol shot. He waited for a moment, listening, and then opened the door and went in. He lit a dark lantern. He found himself in a small kitchen. The door leading out of it was fortunately bolted on his side. He slid back the bolts, top and bottom, and found himself in a narrow passage. Ahead lay the front door, the panes of stained glass on the upper panels gleaming faintly. He remembered that he had entered the waiting-room on the right with Rose and then had gone through to the surgery. There was a door before he reached the waiting-room door, which probably led into the surgery. He tried the handle. It was locked. He hurried along to the waiting-room door. Locked as well. Both were stout mahogany doors. He tried a door on the other side of the corridor. Locked as well.

There was a staircase facing the front door. Perhaps some old files were kept in the upper rooms. Harry crept up the stairs. There were three doors leading off a landing. All were locked.

He retreated to the kitchen, defeated. He could possibly find some implement in the kitchen that might jemmy the door to the surgery open, but that would lead to a full police investigation. All he wanted to do was to read Lord Hedley's file. He sat down for a moment at the kitchen table to rest. Rose was going to be so disappointed in him, he thought with a wry smile.

Perhaps there might be something he could use to pick the lock. But he had never picked a lock before and hadn't the faintest idea of how to go about it.

There was a Welsh dresser against one wall. He set the lantern down on it and opened the first drawer. It was full of knives and forks and spoons. He picked up one of the knives. It had been cleaned so many times with Bath brick that it was thin and fragile. He put it back and opened the other drawer.

At first he could not believe his eyes. He held up the lantern and stared down. The drawer held keys with labels attached.

One label read "Front Door," another "Waiting-Room." There was even one marked "Safe."

Harry grinned and selected the one marked "Surgery." He was about to leave the kitchen when he heard footsteps in the alley outside. He extinguished the lantern and crept to the kitchen door and locked it and then crouched down. The footsteps came closer. A hand rattled the door. Then the footsteps moved on. Glancing up, Harry saw a police helmet bobbing past the window. The constable on his nightly rounds.

He waited and then cautiously relit the lantern and made his way to the surgery and unlocked the door.

He searched along the rows of files, looking for a folder marked "Lord Hedley," but there was nothing there.

It might be in one of the upstairs rooms, thought Harry. I should never have let Rose come. This might take all night and she might do something silly like come looking for me.

He went back to the kitchen and collected the keys to the upstairs rooms. The first had been a bedroom, but the bed was now piled high with odds and ends and the rest of the room was full of discarded furniture.

The next room was an office with a roll-top desk. There were bookshelves all round, full of medical books, some very old indeed. And beside the fire stood a large safe. Harry studied it. To his relief, it was an old-fashioned one without a combination lock. He went back to the kitchen and collected the safe key and went upstairs again.

He unlocked the safe and knelt down in front of it, the lantern on the floor beside him.

There were various items of jewellery in a box: a gold half

hunter, dress studs, a gold Albert and a gold toothpick. Another box contained, to his surprise, an opium pipe and a small quantity of opium. Was Dr. Perriman an opium smoker? Or had that vice been one of the late Dr. Jenner's? There were various title deeds and business papers, and a cash box containing a few hundred pounds.

There was one thick file which he took out and laid on the floor and opened. In it was Lord Hedley's medical file and also correspondence between Dr. Jenner and a Dr. Palverston in London. Harry let out a soundless whistle. The correspondence between the two men discussed the use of arsenic to counteract the effects of syphilis. And in Lord Hedley's file, he found Dr. Jenner had started to treat Lord Hedley for syphilis last summer.

He carefully replaced everything and locked the safe. In order to give Kerridge this information, he would need to cover up the fact that he had broken into the surgery.

He went downstairs and put the keys back in the drawer, being careful to lay them back in the order he had found them.

He breathed a sigh of relief when he locked the kitchen door behind him and hurried off towards where he had left the others in the car.

Daisy and Becket were excited at his news, but Rose seemed a trifle disappointed.

"It all seems so easy," she complained. "I had imagined you having to behave like a real burglar."

Harry had carried that bright image of Rose singing in his car. It popped like a balloon and disappeared. She was really a very silly little girl.

Harry called on Kerridge first thing in the morning with his new information.

"Where did you get this?" demanded the superintendent.

"I can't really tell you."

"You must."

"Superintendent, I know you pay informers and you do not demand where they got their information from and drag them into court."

Kerridge drummed his fingers on the desk. "I can confront Hedley. Even if he admits he has syphilis, he will deny having anything to do with Mary Gore-Desmond. We will then need to approach her parents for further proof—was she sleeping with anyone else?—and that will shake them rigid. But it shows Hedley has arsenic at his disposal.

"Still, I'll need to interview him. You may yet be forced to tell me how you came by this information."

"Let's hope it doesn't come to that," said Harry.

ELEVEN

I had grown weary of him; of his breath
And hands and features I was sick to death.
Each day I heard the same dull voice and tread;
I did not hate him: but I wished him dead.

—G. K. CHESTERTON

Rose had to endure a row from her furious mother. Why had she sent her guard away? Was she misbehaving herself with one of the gentlemen?

Rose protested that the policeman must have misunderstood her. Lady Polly said that they had all been told that they could leave on the following morning.

"I am glad of it. Hedley is not what we had been led to believe. I do not like this extremely vulgar castle and I do not like his guests. That Fairfax woman is atrocious. None of the young men are suitable. We are opening up the town house and the servants have been told to get it ready for our arrival. There will be a few balls and parties before Christmas and, with any luck, you will meet someone suitable there."

"I have decided I do not wish to get married," said Rose.

"What else is there for you to do?"

"I can type. I could get a job."

"Are you out of your mind? Work? You would be a laughing-stock. We do not work!"

And with that, Lady Polly slammed out of her daughter's room in a fury.

Rose felt tears welling up in her eyes and brushed them angrily away. The attempt on her life on the roof was at last beginning to affect her with a bout of delayed shock. She felt weak and useless. Tomorrow they would leave and she would never know what really happened.

Daisy came into the room. "I couldn't help hearing Lady Polly going on at you. So we're going to London."

"It looks like that," said Rose. "I wish I knew who murdered Mary."

"Maybe Miss Bryce-Cuddlestone knows something," said Daisy.

"She won't speak to me."

"Worth a try. Better than doing nothing."

Rose paced up and down and then looked out of the window. "It's a fine, crisp day. I could suggest a walk. Would you take a message to her? If she is agreeable, I will meet her in the hall, in, say, half an hour?"

Rose did not have much hope that Margaret would accept the invitation, but to her surprise Daisy came back and said Margaret had agreed.

Kerridge had summoned Harry. "Not much good," he said. "His lordship was in a fine taking, threatening to have my job."

"Does he admit to having syphilis and possessing arsenic?"

"Not him. 'Prove it, you common little runt' were his last words to me."

"Get a search-warrant."

"I'm trying," said Kerridge bitterly. "I've had orders to release all the guests. I sent a constable to check Dr. Perriman's surgery. No sign of a break-in. How did you do it?"

"I had information from someone."

"You went there yesterday with Lady Rose. Town's still talking about it. Lady Rose and that maid of hers were singing like street balladeers."

"Just a bit of fun."

"Just a bit of distraction while you got up to God knows what. If only something would break. I've more or less been ordered to get out and forget it. The press have given up and gone, so the pressure's off."

"And it's back to hushing the whole thing up?"

"That's it. At least Lord Hedley hasn't stopped repairing the village houses."

"Not yet," said Harry cynically. "I wonder what he'll do when we're all gone."

Rose and Margaret walked in the castle gardens, which were situated to the left of the castle, on the other side from where the tradesmen's entrance was situated.

They had talked generally of fads and fashions, with Daisy and the footman, John, following at a discreet distance behind.

A small pale disk of a sun shone down on the rose garden. Frost still lay on the earth in the shadowy patches which the sun did not reach. Rose half-turned and gave a prearranged signal to Daisy to keep well back and then said in a low voice, "Have you any idea, Miss Bryce-Cuddlestone, who could have committed murder?"

"I don't think it was murder, Lady Rose. I think Mary was a silly girl who just took too much arsenic."

"Then why did your maid end up in the moat?"

"Why should I know?"

"Miss Bryce-Cuddlestone—may I call you Margaret?"

"No."

"Well, then, when you slept with Lord Hedley, did you know he had syphilis?"

"You little bitch! You nasty, snooping little bitch."

"I would like to help. Why? Why did you allow such a man favours?"

"Favours. How old-fashioned." Margaret began to cry, great gulping sobs. Rose put an arm round her and led her to a marble bench. A marble statue of Niobe, shedding marble tears, stared down at them from behind the bench.

Daisy pulled out a handkerchief and handed it to Margaret. She waited patiently until Margaret had gulped and sobbed herself into silence.

"I couldn't bear the idea of another season," said Margaret, in such a low voice that Rose had to bend her head to hear her. "My mother jeers at me a lot. She still fancies herself as a beauty. She is furious with me for already turning down proposals.

"Hedley was fun, not like those dreadful young men. He courted me. He told me that Lady Hedley had a terminal illness and was not expected to live long. He said we would be married and I would be a marchioness and outrank my mother. I slept with him one night, that was all.

"Then Lady Hedley came to my room. She told me about the syphilis. I commiserated with her on her terminal illness, thinking it had turned her brain, but she laughed and said that she was fit and healthy and that her husband should really stop sleeping with virgins because he thought it would cure his illness. I hated him then. I wanted him dead.

"I told her I would expose him, but she laughed. Laughed! She said all I would do would be to broadcast that I was no longer a virgin and that my parents would get to hear of it."

"What did Dr. Perriman say?" asked Rose.

"He said that I showed no sign of the infection. He would not discuss Lord Hedley, but he said that people at the latent stage of the disease were not infectious. They were only infectious in the first and second stages. So I assume I have no fear of the disease developing in me."

"Thank goodness for that. But maybe Mary Gore-Desmond was determined that he should honour his promises. Maybe that's why she had to die."

"But Colette!"

"Perhaps Colette found out somehow and was blackmailing him. You should tell Kerridge."

"No, and if you do, I will deny the whole thing. Lady Hedley puts it about that you are a liar and make things up."

"She does, doesn't she?" said Rose slowly.

Harry burst into the study after luncheon and said to Kerridge, "What fools we've been!"

"Enlighten me."

"Dr. Jenner was in correspondence with a certain Dr. Palverston in London over using arsenic as a treatment. If you confront Dr. Perriman with the fact that we know about the syphilis and the arsenic, he will assume that Dr. Palverston said something. Accuse him of having valuable evidence and threaten to throw the book at him."

"I'll go over to his surgery now," said Kerridge.

Harry went back to his room and rang for Becket. When the manservant appeared, he said, "I want you to keep close to Lady

Rose. I do not want anything to happen to her before we get out of here. I think Hedley could be dangerous and I think his illness is beginning to affect his brain."

Becket went up and knocked at Daisy's door. When she answered it, he said, "The captain says I'm to keep an eye on Lady Rose. Where is she?"

"She said she was going to see Lady Hedley. She's just left."

"Orders are orders. I'd better get down there and wait outside Lady Hedley's sitting-room door."

"We'll both go," said Daisy.

Lady Hedley looked up as Rose entered her sitting-room. "You are supposed to knock," she said crossly. She was still working on the piece of tapestry. "Sit down."

Rose sat down on the other side of the fireplace. Lady Hedley stitched steadily, the needle flashing in and out.

"I came to ask you something," said Rose nervously.

"What?"

Rose was beginning to wish she had not come. The marchioness looked so small and frail.

"I believe your husband takes arsenic for an . . . er . . . illness."

Silence. The needle continued to flash.

"I believe," said Rose, steeling herself, "that he slept with Mary Gore-Desmond sometime at the end of the season because he believed that sleeping with a virgin would cure his illness. I also think Colette knew this and tried to blackmail him. I believe it was he who threw me off the castle roof."

"You are a dangerous and vicious liar," said Lady Hedley. "I love my husband and no one is going to take him from me. You silly young things. What do you know of love?"

Rose stared at her, her mind racing. One of Lady Hedley's lace sleeves fell back as she continued the ply her needle, revealing a surprisingly strong-looking arm.

"I had the money, you see," said the marchioness suddenly. "A chain of grocery shops. You've heard of Crumleys?"

"Yes," said Rose. "I believe the shops are all over the country."

"My father. He rivalled Lipton. But it was trade. I was classed as the daughter of a shopkeeper, no matter how many millions we had. My first season was a nightmare. I was snubbed and patronized all round. It was then that my father, God rest his soul, who was a very shrewd business man, decided to get me a title. His spies told him that Hedley was in debt. Hedley agreed to the marriage, and a good few of those dreadful women who had snubbed me had to watch me take precedence. I did not enjoy the intimate side of marriage and told him to take his pleasures elsewhere, provided he was discreet.

"I believe he went to brothels. But when he contracted syphilis, he began to become foolish. Someone has to look after him," she ended with a sigh. She picked up her needle again.

Rose stared at her. Could it be possible? she wondered. Could the inoffensive-looking Lady Hedley be the strong one in the marriage? If that was the case, then. . . .

She took a chance. "It was you," Rose said. "It was you who murdered Mary Gore-Desmond and killed Colette and tried to kill me."

"But you see, you have no proof and no one will believe you." Lady Hedley continued to stitch at the tapestry just as if Rose had been talking about the weather.

"I will find proof," said Rose.

"But you are leaving tomorrow morning."

"How did you manage to come and go without anyone seeing you?" demanded Rose. "How did you manage to put a drug in the constable's drink? The voice John heard came from below him. So how could you pass him to get at the tea?"

"Simple. The back stairs for the servants are narrow and steep. One of our servants fell down and broke his neck and so after that they were instructed to use the main staircase except when carrying down the slops. I called John, ran up the back stairs and out where he had left the tray. Matter of minutes. I am very resourceful, you know.

"Colette was the worst. Silly woman. She tried to blackmail me. She had seen me on the back stairs the night Mary was poisoned. I told her I would pay her in diamonds but she was to pack her suitcase and meet me outside. I told her I would meet her at the back of the castle because I did not want anyone to see the transaction and the silly fool believed me. So we were standing by the moat and I simply pushed her in. Fortunately she could not swim, although I was fearful the splashing and noise she was making before she drowned would wake someone. The supposed box of diamonds was simply a box with two bricks in it. I put the bricks in her suitcase and threw it in the moat.

"Hedley knew nothing about it. He's a child. He'd ordered so much arsenic from some quack in London, he didn't even know some was missing."

Rose got to her feet. "You are a monster," she said. "I am going straight to Kerridge."

The marchioness ferreted in her work-basket and produced a revolver which she pointed at Rose.

"Sit down," she said. "You are not going anywhere until I decide what to do with you."

Rose stayed standing. The light from the fire shone red on the barrel of the wicked-looking revolver.

Her knees were shaking, but she said, "I am going to walk out of here and you are not going to stop me. You cannot shoot me."

The marchioness rose as well and walked around the tapestry stand to face Rose. "I can shoot you and put the gun in your hand and say you committed suicide. Everyone will believe me because you are regarded as odd."

The door swung open and Daisy darted into the room and flung herself in front of Rose just as Lady Hedley fired.

The bullet hit Daisy in the side. But Daisy had inherited Rose's steel-boned corsets and the bullet ricocheted off one of the steels, pinged off a bronze bust of Lord Hedley, and planted itself in the marchioness's forehead.

Becket was shouting, "Police!" at the top of his voice.

Footmen and police came bounding up the stairs. The marchioness was lying on the rug by the fire, a hole in her forehead and her brains spilling out the back of her head over the rug.

Daisy had fainted. While Becket was rapidly explaining that he and Daisy had heard Lady Hedley's confession, Rose ripped open Daisy's muslin blouse. "Get me scissors," she shouted.

A policeman handed her a pair of scissors from the work-basket and Rose cut the lacing on the stays and pulled them apart. There was no blood. She began to cry with shock and relief.

Then Harry was there with his arms around her, helping her to her feet.

"I don't care if it's a cover-up," said Kerridge wearily early that evening. He and Harry were closeted in the study. "The criminal is dead and so I don't mind bowing to pressure. The story is this. Lady Hedley took her own life while the balance of her

mind was disturbed. Mary Gore-Desmond's death was accidental. Colette? Who cares about a blackmailing French maid who
doesn't seem to have any family that we can trace?"

"So who knows the truth?"

"Just you, Becket, Daisy and Rose. Oh, and Rose's parents.
A couple of footmen. Do you know Lady Polly's reaction? She
said, 'Do you mean that maid saved my daughter's life? Oh,
dear, we'll need to keep her now. She knows too much and she
knows about the other business.' What other business, Captain
Cathcart?"

"Haven't the faintest," lied Harry, for he knew Rose's mother
had been referring to the bombing at Stacey Magna. "How is
Lady Rose? I haven't been allowed to see her."

"Remarkably well, considering everything. She's a brave girl.
If it hadn't been for her we'd probably never have found out."

"If it hadn't been for Daisy, she'd probably be dead. How is
Daisy?"

"Chirpy as a Cockney sparrow. The doctor says she has a
huge bruise under where the bullet hit the steel. Oh, that was
something else Lady Polly found to complain about. She asked
Lady Rose, 'What were you doing giving an expensive corset
to your maid?'"

"So Lady Rose starts to complain that she cannot abide the
constriction of that sort of stays and they end up having an
argument about dress."

"How's Hedley?"

"He's trying to look shocked, but you can see it's dawning
on him that he gets all her money. He'll be able to buy his
virgins, now. What a world. I suppose you've turned out not to
be any use to Hedley."

"On the contrary, I am employed to go about the sordid
business of making sure the footmen on the scene keep their

mouths shut. I suggested it might be a good idea to bribe Daisy. No one apart from Rose is thanking her and I feel she deserves a reward."

"What will you do with your life now?" asked Kerridge.

"I'm not quite sure," said Harry, bending down and rubbing his bad leg. "But next time, I will be sure that the people I work for are decent and honourable."

"Captain, if they were decent and honourable, they would not require your services. You've heard of Pinkerton's National Detective Agency, haven't you?"

"Of course."

"You might try something like that. Get something maybe a bit more meaty than blowing up railways stations all because some earl doesn't want to entertain the king."

"I haven't the faintest idea what you're talking about. There's the dressing gong." Harry held out his hand. "It's been a pleasure meeting you. I don't suppose we'll meet again."

Kerridge shook his hand. "I'm sure we will, Captain. I'm sure we will."

Harry had assumed that Lord Hedley would not be present at the dinner table, but there he was at the head as usual. He was wearing a black armband, as were the other men there. The ladies had all found something black to wear.

To his surprise, Rose was there as well, her face looking pale and almost translucent above the black of her dress.

Conversation was muted, but as the wine circulated, voices began to rise. "So awful," said Maisie Chatterton to Harry. Harry was amused to notice that all the drama had made Maisie forget to lisp. "But I always thought there was something a little bit mad about her. I never want to come here again."

"I think we'll all be glad to leave in the morning," said Harry.

Miss Fairfax's voice boomed out, "I think it's all very fishy. No one will tell me quite what happened. I was talking to Lady Hedley the other day and she seemed happy and well."

There was a shocked silence. Then Sir Gerald said, "Now, my precious, you mustn't be so tactless. It makes your eyes narrow, and we don't want that, now do we?"

To Harry's amazement, Miss Fairfax gave a giggle and rapped Gerald on the arm with her fan. "Naughty, *naughty* boy."

She really must have an awful lot of money, thought Harry cynically. He glanced again at Rose, who was listlessly picking at her food. Did she feel like him, a misfit? He had been more comfortable in the company of Kerridge than in the fellowship of his peers.

Upstairs, Becket knocked at the door of Daisy's room and crept in. He glanced at the inner door which connected Daisy's room with Rose's and whispered, "Is she in there?"

"Gone down to dinner." Daisy was lying propped up against the pillows, a bound copy of *Young England* on her lap and a box of chocolates on the table beside the bed.

Becket drew up a chair and sat down next to her. "Did you get your pay-off?"

"One hundred guineas. Did you get the same?"

Becket nodded.

"Going to leave the captain?"

"Never. What about you? You could buy a shop."

"No, I'll stick with Lady Rose. She needs me. If we're going to run away to London, she'll need some money and so will I."

"Thank goodness you had those corsets on."

"She'd just given them to me, too. She hates them, but I felt so grand even though they were uncomfortable. Choc?"

"Thanks," said Becket, picking one out. "Someone's coming

along the corridor. They've stopped outside the door."

"Get into the bed," said Daisy, whipping back the covers.

There was a knock at the door. "Come in," called Daisy.

Curzon, the butler, walked in. "I know the true story of how you saved your mistress's life. I have always said that breeding will out. I would like you to accept this as a token of my esteem." He held out a carved cigarette-box.

"Thank you," said Daisy in a weak voice because Becket's body under the covers was crammed against her own and she wanted Curzon to go.

To her relief, the butler said, "I can see that you are still very shocked. Be always assured that your secret is safe with me."

"Thank you."

Daisy waited until she heard Curzon's footsteps go along the corridor and down the steps and then she whipped back the covers. "Get out of here!"

"I wasn't doing anything," complained Becket. "I was suffocating. Any cigarettes in that box?"

Daisy opened the lid and sniffed. "Turkish. The best."

"Let's have one, then. Do you smoke?"

"Now and then."

He lit cigarettes for both of them. "Will you write to me?" he asked.

"Yes, I can write now," said Daisy proudly.

"Aren't you going to give some of that money to your family?"

"Naw! Da would drink it all. So would Ma, come to think of it. Oh, maybe I'll go down there and see if I can slip something to the children."

"Daisy, do you think that one day, maybe one day, we—"

The inner door opened and Rose walked in. "You should not be here, Becket," she said. "I think Daisy deserves to enjoy your company, but if my mother should find you here, I would be in more trouble than I am already. And smoking, as well!"

Becket left. Daisy began to get up. "No, stay where you are," said Rose. "I can put myself to bed. My parents' servants have packed most of our things, so you do not need to exert yourself."

"You'll be glad to get out of here," said Daisy.

"Yes, of course I will. Good night."

Rose trailed off to her own room and sat down at the dressing-table. Back to London tomorrow. No more frights and alarms, no more Kerridge and his policemen, no more Captain Harry Cathcart. Why did life suddenly feel so flat?

EPILOGUE

There's something undoubtedly in a fine air,
To know how to smile and be able to stare,
High breeding is something, but well-bred or not,
In the end the one question is, what have you got.
So needful it is to have money, heigh-ho!
So needful it is to have money.

And the angels in pink and the angels in blue,
In muslins and moirés so lovely and new,
What is it they want, and so wish you to guess,
But if you have money, the answer is Yes.
So needful, they tell you, is money, heigh-ho!
So needful it is to have money.

–A. H. CLOUGH

The next morning, everyone was up early. Everyone seemed so glad to get out of the castle at last.

Lady Polly was fussing about her daughter as a footman helped Rose into the carriage. Rose knew her parents were feeling extremely guilty at having sent her to the castle in the first place, and she hoped to work on that guilt when they got to London.

Rose looked out of the carriage window. Harry was just emerging from the castle, pulling on his driving gloves. Infuriating man. Perhaps if she went to some parties in London he might be there. It would be pleasant to let him know just how infuriating he was.

"What I don't like," grumbled the earl as the carriage jolted forwards, "is Hedley being so cheerful about getting his wife's money."

"He won't live long to enjoy it," said Rose. "The syphilis is already beginning to eat up his appearance."

"That's enough of that," snapped the earl. "A young girl should not know of such things."

"Maybe if Mary Gore-Desmond had known of such things she would still be alive," retorted Rose.

"Don't speak to your father like that," said Lady Polly. "I know your poor nerves are overset by your dreadful experience, but there is no need for you to be so . . . coarse."

The Peterson sisters were driven off in their motor car while Miss Fairfax followed in her carriage, accompanied by Sir Gerald.

"Faster," Harriet urged the chauffeur. "I want to leave her behind. We really need to write to Mother, Debs, and get her off our backs. She was bad enough before, but she'll ruin our chances, twittering and ogling with that awful creature on her arm."

"Goodbye, rotten castle," said Deborah, as the car rolled over the drawbridge. "As I told you, there was something fishy about Lady Hedley shooting herself. Rose was there. I tried to ask her this morning but her mother interrupted and pulled her away. Also, I sent my maid over to Creinton for some ribbons and she told me that Captain Harry, Rose and their servants were singing in the street. For money!"

"Can't have been them. The Earl of Hadshire is most frightfully rich."

"Ah, but the captain's reported to have very little over his army pension," said Deborah. "It must be so demeaning to be poor. He should marry Rose. I mean, her parents should be glad to get anyone for her now."

"Oh, that scandal about Blandon will be over and forgotten. She's got money and a title and looks. She won't stay on the shelf for long," said Harriet.

"You know what I think?" Deborah clutched her hat as the car swung out onto the main road. "I think Rose is the type to make things happen. Mark my words, she'll be embroiled in another scandal before Christmas."

"I hear her parents are shipping her off to India."

"Well, all I can say is poor India," said Deborah. "She'll start another mutiny or something."

Freddy Pomfret and Tristram Baker-Willis and their valets were deposited at Creinton Railway Station by one of the castle carriages.

"Absolutely poisonous visit," complained Freddy, listlessly poking the fire in the first-class waiting-room. "Deaths and shootings. Boring melodrama. Like being trapped between the covers of one of Mrs. Henry Wood's novels."

"And that Rose creature," said Tristram. "Getting us into trouble. That Trumpington woman was leering at us in the most horrible way. Turns my stomach to think of it."

Freddy produced a silver flask. "Here. Have a swig of this. I filled it up with Hedley's brandy."

Tristam took the flask from him and downed a great swallow. "That's better. We didn't have a chance with the Peterson girls after that. Tell you what. Lady Rose is going to London. Let's think up some way to get even."

The waiting room began to shake under the thunder of the approaching train. "Here we go," said Freddy. "London, here we come."

Margaret Bryce-Cuddlestone, accompanied by the Trumpingtons, stared bleakly out of the window. The landscape was white, in the grip of a severe hoar-frost.

She could only be grateful that she had escaped with her reputation intact. She did not believe for a moment the reasons given for Lady Hedley's taking her own life. Remembering her talk with Rose, she was sure that somehow Rose had found out that Lady Hedley was a murderess and had challenged her. Thank goodness it was being hushed up or she might have had to appear in the dock as a witness. The whole experience had shaken her. She could only pray that she was not pregnant. Her menstruation was not due until the following week.

In that moment, Margaret made up her mind. She would stop looking for love and this time she would accept the proposal of the first man who asked her to marry him.

Mrs. Trumpington nudged her husband awake. "I wonder if I should go to India with the Hadshires' gel. There's something unstable about her. At first I thought, well, jolly good, free holiday and all that. Bit of travel. But the more I think about it, the less I like it. I mean, heat and flies and Rose likely to get embroiled in something awful. This suffragette business! She's just the sort to go around campaigning for equal rights for the Indians and befriending the untouchables. Then one has to think of the distance and socializing with all those frightfully boring memsahibs. No, I won't go. You'd miss me, wouldn't you, dear?"

"What? What?"

"I said, you'd miss me."

"Yes, yes," grumbled Mr. Trumpington. "Now can I go back to sleep?"

Miss Fairfax and Gerald sat holding hands. "I am so glad I met you," she said.

"I'm amazed a charming lady like yourself never married," said Gerald, gazing into her eyes and mentally paying off his tailor's bills.

"Oh, I had my chances. But would you believe it? The men in Virginia are every bit as mercenary as they are here. Not you, of course, dear heart."

"You had to fight off adventurers?"

"On my poor little dowry?"

"My poppet, everyone knows your family is extremely rich."

"That's my sister, Clarrie. She did well. Married Burton, who is rolling in railroad money. She's paying for my trip to London and all my expenses."

Gerald felt as if a cold dark stone had settled in his stomach. He tried to pull his hand away but she held it in a firm grip.

Clive Fraser, Bertram Brookes, Harry Trenton and Neddie Fee-mantle had only journeyed as far as the village pub. Drawn together by a feeling of failure, they set about getting drunk. Each had hoped to become engaged to one of the American sisters and put the sisters' obvious lack of interest in any of them down to the odd happenings at the castle.

They got so drunk and obnoxious that the landlord had to send a message to the castle appealing to the marquess to come and get rid of them.

The remaining ladies, equally disappointed, were heading to-wards London. Perhaps each in her way was more shocked by the happenings than Rose. For a brief spell their lives, which had been as well-padded by wealth and class as their fashionable hourglass figures, had been invaded by a darker world. Maisie Chatterton and Lady Sarah Trenton longed for the bright lights and shops of London. Frederica Sutherland planned to stay only two days in London before journeying to her home in Scotland.

Maisie Chatterton decided she would never lisp again. Her mother had told her that men were fascinated by a girlish lisp, but all they did was to stare at her and then ask her to repeat what she had just said.

Lady Sarah planned to hint at the horror of the dark hap-penings at the castle and at the next ball conveniently swoon into the arms of the most handsome man present.

Frederica Sutherland was determined to convince her par-ents that there was no need for her ever to go south again, no need for her to leave her beloved dogs and horses.

She turned in the carriage and looked back at Castle Telby standing up square and bleak against the winter sky. She considered herself a jolly good sort, good at hunting and shooting, better than the men. She could not wait to get out of these frippery clothes and get some decent tweeds on again.

Harry felt quite low as Becket unlocked the door of the house in Water Street. His leg was hurting and he put it down to that. Becket went upstairs to unpack Harry's bags and Harry lit the fire in his front parlour and settled down with a glass of sherry.

He felt almost angry with Rose at having hit on a solution to the murders and nearly getting herself killed. He was the detective. He was the one who should have hit on a solution to the mystery.

He rose and picked up his mail and began to sift through it. There was one from a Mrs. Debenham asking him if he could find her lost poodle. Is this all his intelligence was capable of, while some silly, unfeminine female went around solving murders?

Becket came in carrying his slippers.

"Pour yourself a glass of sherry, Becket, and sit down. I feel like company." Becket poured a glass and sat down on the other side of the fireplace.

"I don't think I should go on with this stupid detective business, Becket. What do you think?"

"It is not my place to say, sir."

"Just this once, make it your place."

"If I may say so, sir, you were doing very well and we

have comforts such as the motor car which we did not have before."

"I could travel. Find some work in the colonies."

Then I really won't see Daisy again, thought Becket.

"You said, sir, that Superintendent Kerridge had suggested you might start a proper detective agency. Should you do that, you would maybe be given more interesting work. The insurance companies, for example, must always be looking for investigators."

"I feel I, and not Lady Rose, should have hit on the solution to what had been going on at the castle."

"That was just luck on Lady's Rose's part. And just think! Had you not told me to keep guard on Lady Rose, she would be dead."

Harry brightened slightly. "That's true."

"I could look for suitable premises tomorrow," suggested Becket.

"Let me think about it."

Just before Christmas, Rose finally agreed to attend a ball at the Cummings' with her mother. Lady Polly was worried about her daughter. Ever since they had arrived in London from the castle, Rose had appeared tired and listless.

"Cheer up," said Daisy as she arranged silk flowers in Rose's hair. "Captain Cathcart might be there and you can talk about old times."

"Those times are not yet old enough for my comfort. I would like to forget about the whole thing. Do you think this yellow is unflattering?"

Rose was wearing a yellow sateen evening gown embroidered with tiny yellow primroses and with inserts of white lace.

"It's a pretty gown but you are a bit pale," said Daisy. "Maybe a touch of rouge?"

"No."

"What about this idea of us being businesswomen? I read the advertisements every day."

"Oh, that was a silly idea, Daisy. I would never be allowed to do it. This is my life from now on. I may as well settle for some amiable man and then at least I would have my own establishment."

Daisy bit back a sigh. She thought it would be wonderful to have a life filled with nothing but balls and parties and pretty dresses. She opened the curtains and looked down into the square. "Fog's coming down. Going to be nasty. I'd better have that dress shut away when we get back. When it's a bad one, the fog gets in everywhere."

By the time Lady Polly had fussed over her daughter's appearance and made her change her evening bag and gloves several times, they were late leaving, and what Dickens had called a London particular had settled down on the city.

"Thank goodness we haven't got far to go," said Lady Polly as the carriage rolled the short distance to Belgrave Square. "I can hardly see a thing out of the windows."

"I hate knee-breeches," grumbled the earl. "Silly things. Ought to be confined to court appearances. With my figure, I feel I look like Humpty Dumpty."

"You look very fine, my dear," said Lady Polly.

Surely her parents had married for love, thought Rose. Lady Polly never found any fault with her husband. Rose had seen photographs of their wedding day. Her father had been a slim, handsome man then, and she was sure that was how her mother still saw him.

The coach lurched to a stop. Extra footmen hired for the evening lined the entrance. "I wonder how you clean all that gold braid after the fog," wondered Daisy. "Must ask Becket." Then she remembered there was no Becket to ask and felt quite low.

In an ante-room reserved for the ladies, Daisy removed Rose's fur coat and checked that her hair was still in order and that none of the little silk primroses in it had come loose. Bands of fog lay across the ante-room.

Rose mounted the staircase to the ballroom where their hosts appeared at the top through thickening layers of fog.

"So kind of you to come out on such a dreadful night," murmured Mrs. Cummings.

To Lady Polly's relief, her daughter's dance-card was soon filled up. The scandal appeared to have been forgotten.

Rose had given up the idea of trying to engage any of her partners in intelligent conversation and so was a great success.

Harry had decided to attend the ball. He would not admit to himself that he hoped Rose would be there. His white shirt-front well protected against the choking fog, he motored alone to Belgrave Square, having told Becket there was no need to accompany him and failing to notice the look of disappointment on Becket's face.

He mounted the steps to the ballroom with an unusual feeling of anticipation. As he was late, his hosts had joined their guests. He surveyed the room where the dancers twirled in a waltz and sent the wreaths of fog spiralling about them.

"Captain Cathcart!"

He looked down and found Lady Polly beside him.

"Good evening," said Harry happily. "I trust your daughter is well."

"Very well and engaged for every dance. It would be better if you did not approach her. She has not been well in spirit since the dreadful events at the castle. I beg you to leave her alone."

"Certainly," said Harry coldly.

Rose danced past in the arms of a handsome guardsman. She saw him and her eyes widened.

Harry turned on his heel and walked back down the stairs. He should never have come. His leg was hurting. It looked as if it was going to be a bad winter. He would go somewhere warm and decide what to do with his life.

A footman was helping him into his fur coat when Daisy appeared at his side. "Why, Daisy," said Harry, "how are you?"

"I'm all right," said Daisy, "but my mistress is not the same. She's so sad and quiet. Where's Becket?" she asked eagerly, looking around.

"Becket is in Chelsea. I will tell him I saw you."

"Are you doing any more detective work, sir?"

"No. In fact I have just decided I have had enough of London weather. I crave some sunshine. I think I will take myself off to Nice."

"Where's that?"

"The south of France, Daisy."

"And will you take Becket with you?"

"Of course. We could both do with some good weather."

"Tell Mr. Becket I wish him well," said Daisy and trailed off.

The ball finished early because of the dreadful weather. As Rose and her parents stood on the steps waiting for the carriage to be brought round, snow began to fall through the filthy fog, great lacy flakes.

The earl let out a rattling cough. "My dear, your chest!" exclaimed Lady Polly. "Pull your scarf up round your throat. Thank goodness. Here's our carriage."

Rose sat silently in her corner of the carriage. Why hadn't Harry spoken to her? It would have only been polite. They had been through so much together. She felt jaded and weary and a large tear rolled down her cheek.

Lady Polly saw that tear in the dim light of the carriage lamp and let out a squawk of dismay. "You are never crying, Rose. You were such a success."

"I am not feeling very well," lied Rose.

Lady Polly fussed over her daughter while Daisy prepared her for bed. Then she told the maid to come with her.

Daisy followed Lady Polly's sturdy little figure to the countess's sitting-room.

"Is my daughter really ill?" demanded Lady Polly. "Should we send for the doctor?"

"I think Lady Rose is suffering from delayed shock," said Daisy. A bright idea dawned in her head.

"I think what Lady Rose, and, if I may be so bold, the master need is some sunshine."

"We are due to leave for Stacey next week," said Lady Polly impatiently, "and there isn't any sunshine there."

"I was thinking of Nice, my lady. That's in the south of France."

"I know where it is. My old friend, Gertie Robbald, lives permanently in the Imperial Hotel."

"Sea air and sunshine," cooed Daisy, "would do Lady Rose the world of good."

"You may be right. But we always have Christmas at Stacey."

The earl came in at that moment, coughing and wheezing. "It's too bad," he said. "Brum tells me the factor phoned and two of the pipes have burst at Stacey and the drawing-room is flooded."

"Run along," Lady Polly ordered Daisy.

Daisy went outside the door and pressed her ear to the panels.

"I have had an idea," said Lady Polly. "We don't want to go back to a freezing, flooded house. I am worried about your chest and about poor Rose being so frail. Why don't we go to Nice? Gertie's there, at the Imperial. We could get some sunshine and sea air."

"Be funny not celebrating Christmas in England," said the earl.

"It would be awful celebrating Christmas in this filthy weather. Oh, do say yes. Only think of poor Rose."

"I suppose it wouldn't do any harm. I'll get my secretary to make the arrangements."

Daisy darted back up the stairs to Rose's bedchamber. Rose was lying in bed, reading a book.

"We're going to Nice!" said Daisy, pirouetting around the room.

"What? When?"

"As soon as possible. Just think! Sunshine and adventures."

Rose smiled at her maid's enthusiasm. "I'm glad you're happy. Why should they decide on Nice?"

Daisy looked at her. If she told Rose about Captain Cathcart, Rose might tell her mother and then they wouldn't go.

"Dunno," she said.